PERIWINKLE

AND OTHER SHORT STORIES.

TARA GOPINATH

Made with ❤ on the Notion Press Platform
www.notionpress.com

Dedicated to,

Friends and Well Wishers

Contents

FOREWORD

Rekha Rai, M.A., Head of the Department of English (Retd.)
MES Degree College, Bangalore.

"Periwinkle", an attractive bouquet of short stories, written by Tara Gopinath, presents a window to her world view which is genial, generous and very positive. Her short stories are characterized by men and women of rare grit and determination, yet very gentle and humane. Tara's keen powers of observation and eye for detail truly make each short story unique and highly interesting. Simple incidents, drawn from everyday life, tinged with humour and an easy narrative style, sets each short story apart, and engages the reader every step of the way.

I found the short stories delightful and I consider it a privilege to write the foreword to "Periwinkle", Tara's collection of short stories. I wish that "Periwinkle" is the precursor of many more collections of short stories.

PREFACE

Dear Readers,

It's my pleasure to present to you the English version of my Marathi short-story book, 'Periwinkle'.

Pleasure – just one word, but it has several shades. With God's blessings and my luck, I could experience many of those; the satisfaction of writing a story – the excitement when it gets published – the happiness when readers respond and – and finally the joy when the stories are published collectively in a book.

Living in a cosmopolitan city like Bengaluru, I have multilingual friends. Many of them were keen to read stories from my first short story book 'Periwinkle', which was published on 29th January 2024. However, since those stories were written in Marathi, they "demanded" its English translation; naturally out of their love and affection. Thanks a million, my dear friends, for your encouragement. Your kind reminders were of great importance to me! Because of you, I have the pleasure of publishing the English version of 'Periwinkle'.

Writing a story is an individual effort, but publishing a book is a joint venture. Hence, I would like to express my sincere gratitude to each one of them who helped me in this endeavour.

First of all, I would like to thank my daughter-in-law, Trupti Rao. Though the thought of translating my stories into English lingered in my mind after publishing 'Periwinkle' in Marathi, it was converted into action only after Trupti pitched in. I cherish the pleasent memories of working with her on this book. She set the ball rolling and prepared the first draft of the English translation. After that, there was no looking back. I am immensely thankful to her.

My sincere thanks to Mrs. Rekha Rai- M.A., Head of Department of English (Retd.), MES Degree College, Bangalore, who gracefully accepted to write the 'Foreword' to my book and reviewed the manuscript. My niece Dr. Nirupama Joshi helped with the tedious job of editing. Mrs. Ratna Rao – Trainer, Teacher and Author, helped with the process of self-publishing and wrote a review too. Mr. Pratik Kate, the artist, drew apt pictures for each story, and designed the attractive cover. My family members Mr. Gopinath, Sundip and Trupti, Sudhir and Beena, whole-heartedly supported the idea. And last but not the least, the NOTION PRESS cooperated at every stage and printed the book.

By profession, my better half Mr. Gopinath and I are Architects and we had a Consultancy Firm by name Gopinath and Katakam. During 25 years of private practice, I designed Hotels, Hospitals, Resorts, Apartments, Villas and Residences. I had immense joy and satisfaction when those were completed and inaugurated. After retirement, both of us pursued our hobbies, travelled widely - in India as well as abroad - and I enjoyed writing travelogues of those visits.I also wrote short stories which were published in Marathi magazines.

I am a member of International Inner Wheel – an NGO, and I led the Inner Wheel District 319, as District Chairman for one year. I am also an active member of Maharashtra Mandal and Stree Sakhi and participate in their programs.

In this journey of life, I witnessed many incidents that engraved a mark in my memory and I came across a variety of persons who enriched my life. I would be happy if my stories kindled your memories too. However, if you relate to some characters in the story or recollect an incident in your life while reading my stories; it's just a coincidence, as all the characters and incidents in the stories are purely fictional.

I do hope that you enjoy reading this book, as much as I enjoyed writing it...

Thank you.

Tara Gopinath.

30 March 2025, Gudhipadva.

Note By Translator

Enter Caption

"Translating Periwinkle was a truly enriching experience, and I am grateful to my mother-in-law Tara Gopinath for giving me this opportunity. Initially, I assumed translation would be a straightforward task, but as I delved deeper, I realized the true challenge lay in capturing the essence of idioms and cultural nuances that often lacked direct English equivalents. This journey has deepened my appreciation for the richness of the Marathi language and its subtleties. I hope the translated stories resonate with a wider audience, allowing them to experience and appreciate the soulful, varied and heart-warming stories written by Tara Gopinath."

Trupti Rao.

REVIEW

'Periwinkle' offers a delectable collection of "slice of life" stories. The author, Tara Gopinath, is a keen observer of human behaviour and depicts small but meaningful experiences with warmth and kindness.

We are easily drawn into the world of Jaya the chatterbox, Selvan the groom and the petrified Vasu, to name a few. 'Periwinkle' being a translation of her own book in Marathi, the writing is friendly and earnest, and this makes each story feel real.

We come across familiar settings of revived friendships, bustling apartments, school traumas – and read about simple touching events. With no dramatic twists or exaggerated plots, this is a book that lingers in your mind long after you have put it down. A hot cup of tea, and this book, is what you need when you wish to relax.

Ratna Rao, Teacher, Trainer and Author

I
Donation

It's very normal for the residents of our Housing Society to see
a transport truck standing in the podium - because every now and

then - some family, out of 1630 apartments housed in 17 residential towers - would be either moving in or moving out of our Society.

And yet on that day, when I returned from my morning walk and noticed a truck of "Movers and Packers" unloading luggage in front of our building, I was surprised. Because it was the month of *Ashadh* (as per the lunar calendar)– the month in which shifting of residence was generally avoided. In fact, let alone shifting, no one would even come to inspect an empty apartment during the month of *Ashadh*...So, questions like 'who and why' about the new tenants kept my mind occupied till I reached home. But I didn't have to wait for long to get the answers. On the third day, our doorbell rang.

As I peeped through the side window, I saw a man in his fifties, wearing a safari suit, standing there.

"Namaste." He said with folded hands and a broad smile on his face. "I am Maganbhai Thakkar. Just two days back we shifted to your building. It's good to know neighbours, isn't it? So, I have come to introduce myself."

"Oh, nice. Please come inside and have a seat." I said and opened the door. "My husband will join you in a minute." Saying so, I went in to prepare some tea.

Since ours is an open kitchen, I could hear their conversation very clearly. In that first meeting itself Maganbhai told everything about his immediate family and extended family, their businesses etc. He also shared the additional information as to why he shifted in *Ashadh* month. It seems his apartment owner agreed to reduce the rent by 2% if he shifts in the *Ashadh* month itself, so Maganbhai accepted that deal and moved in the *Ashadh* month.

As I brought the tray with tea and biscuits, he exclaimed, "Oh, I should have told you before itself not to add sugar in my tea... I mean, I don't have diabetes, but it's better to avoid sugar, isn't it? Actually even you should avoid tea with sugar..." And then he gave us a brief 20 minute explanation on 'how money can be saved throughout the year just by reducing sugar in tea. Besides sugar expenses, doctors' bills, medicine expenses are also saved and the bonus is good health.' He said vehemently. " Of course, both of you look healthy, but care is better than cure, isn't it?" he said the parting sentence and left.

He made us think, – no, not the sour thought of going sugarless! We were taken aback by the overdose of knowledge poured in our heads in that very first meeting from our brand-new neighbour. Though we decided to keep a respectable distance from Maganbhai, we kept meeting him very often - mostly in the lift. Soon he came to know that his grandmother's and my native place were the same. So, he started addressing me as 'Chachi' and my husband as 'Chacha'. He started visiting us often and several times invited us to his house too.

I remember distinctly when I visited his house for the first time. The living room was so crowded with furniture - that too - assorted furniture. Cane moda, plush recliner, steel sofa, carved Kashmiri teapoy, plastic chair, and wooden dewan, all brushing shoulders with each other. Watching the confused expression on my face, his wife said,

"Chachi, you can sit wherever you will be comfortable." Then as if reading my mind, she explained proudly, "We have a variety of furniture because my husband buys it only when there is a 'sale' and he gets a good deal. It saves a lot of money, isn't it?"

"Yes, that's true" I replied, and swallowed the question "but what about some uniformity?"

After that visit I realized that- unlike most of us- he was tight-fisted when it came to spending money on himself, that the major goal of his life was to save money at any cost and they would compromise anything for that...

However, one thing was remarkable about Maganbhai. He was always ready to help others. Not only his own money, but Maganbhai was keen on saving other people's money also by guiding them and helping them to buy anything and everything – from fridge to safety pins – at discounted rates from one of his friend's or relative's shop! Naturally, everybody sought his advice before any purchase. Besides that, he helped some people to claim Health Insurance money and for some others he even got authentic

Gujarati snacks.

^^^^^^^^^^^^^^^^^^^^^^

Gradually Maganbhai became popular in the Society. He became an integral part of our community and was invited for every function by the residents. That day, we had gathered at the Club House for the birthday party of Mr. Gundgol's five-year-old son. The children gathered around the beautifully decorated cake and sang the 'Happy Birthday' song. Mrs. Gundgol removed the lit candles and kept it aside in a candle stand, because she believed that putting off the candle flame was inauspicious. Then the cake was cut by the birthday boy and was distributed along with some other snacks to the guests. Like children, we too enjoyed the treat and the light-hearted chat with each other.

And suddenly we heard Maganbhai's voice. He was talking to Mr. Gundgol. We couldn't stop ourselves from overhearing their conversation. Maganbhai asked whether Mr. Gundgol had taken any Life Insurance Policy for his son. If not, then he should; because for a child, the premium would be very minimum, so he must make at least 25 Lakh rupees worth of policy. He also said that he himself was an LIC agent and he would help with all the paperwork. Then he concluded with, "See you tomorrow at your apartment... I am telling you all this, because one should be prepared for every eventuality. Nobody can predict the future and we don't know what will happen and when..."

Maganbhai left along with his granddaughter, but spoiled the happy mood of Mr. Gundgol and his wife. We also felt embarrassed. The question mark on everybody's face read, "How could he broach a subject like that on this occasion? Was Maganbhai totally unaware that on a happy occasion like a birthday celebration, even the mere mention of death could be traumatic to the family members...?"

^^^^^^^^^^^^^^^^^^^^^^^^^^^^

After that incident, it started happening all the time. Basically, renting an apartment in our society seemed like a calculated move by Mr. Maganbhai Thakkar. A Society with 1630 apartments... Even if he gets only one policy per family, how much of commission he would earn from that ... He was already a millionaire and dreamt of becoming a multi-millionaire. He started attending all the events in the society without fail, and started selling LIC policies suitable for everyone, - be it christening or housewarming... from a nine-day old baby to a ninety-year-old great grandpa... Maganbhai always had an appropriate LIC scheme for them. No matter how the train of conversation started with the host family, he always ended it at his favorite stop- with his favorite tagline: "We don't know what will happen when..."

Of course, nothing was wrong in that, because everyone knew the importance of Insurance. In fact, many of us had already invested in various LIC policies. However, on an auspicious occasion, when Maganbhai brought up the subject of Insurance people used to get upset. The mention of death dampened the celebration spirit.

His stinginess became another reason for avoiding him. No one could convince him or argue with him on money-matters. He would refuse to contribute anything for any of the festivals or pooja celebrated in the Society, saying that he gathers enough "PUNYA" by feeding half a kilo organic grain to the pigeons every day. Though this act created a pigeon menace in the society, according to him, that was his good deed.

Well, the donation was voluntary, but he wouldn't pay even the Society Maintenance Charge within the stipulated time frame. He always paid it on the last day. The reason was that the longer the maintenance amount remained in his own bank account, it would earn more interest in his account.

Gradually Maganbhai became the subject of ridicule and sneer due to his stubbornness, and miserly nature. As steadily as it grew, his popularity faded in due course of time.

∧∧∧∧∧∧∧∧∧∧∧∧∧∧∧∧

... And then one day, the news came that Maganbhai had a fall in the bathroom, had hurt his head badly, and was in the ICU of a hospital.

As so called 'Chacha-Chachi', it was our duty to at least - visit him in the hospital - but we didn't go – in fact, no one did.

In a week's time, another news came... Maganbhai had passed away due to severe bleeding in the brain... Just one fall and Maganbhai was no more... It was hard to believe...

We kept remembering his favorite tagline: "We don't know what will happen and when... " How true!!!

Maganbhai's lifeless body was laid on the podium. Many residents had come to pay homage to the departed soul. One of them asked Maganbhai's son, as to when and where the cremation would be, so that we would go there. His answer stunned us. Looking at his dead body, we just stood there – speechless - with a numb mind - and moist eyes...

Maganbhai Thakkar was not to be cremated.

Because as per Maganbhai's wish, the useful organs from his body were to be transplanted in needy patients, and the rest of the body was to be donated to a medical college...

Six ailing patients were to get a 'new lease of life' because of Maganbhai...

What an extraordinary donation... donating his whole body...

Maganbhai Thakkar, whom we had labelled as the 'Most Miserly Donor', was in reality 'the Donor of the Highest Order'.

* *

* * * * * * * * * * * * * * * *

II
Millie

"OH, - come on Laura, at least for once try to understand his feelings..." I was aware of my rising voice. Generally, I don't lose my cool, but that day the situation was different. Laura was not at all in the listening mode. Instead, she kept on ranting the same thing again and again. I was seething with anger. Finally, Laura said quietly, "...Pooja, if you care so much for his feelings, ... why don't you marry him?... I don't mind."

"Yes, I would have certainly married him, ... but, how can I? ...he is in love with you..." I retorted. I knew my anger was rising. I was afraid that if I continued to convince her any further, I might cross the line of friendship, so I hung up the phone straight away.

∧∧∧∧∧∧∧∧∧∧∧∧∧∧∧∧∧∧∧∧

Pooja

With a degree in 'Hotel Management' from Manipal College, I too aspired to study further in America- like some of my other batchmates- and joined Denton University in Texas. I was not particularly interested in catering, but had a strong desire to advance my education in the Hospitality sector. The college fees were covered by the scholarship I received, and for other expenses, Dad took a loan from the bank. I was very money conscious and avoided unnecessary expenses keeping to myself and my studies. I had no friends and no place to go. That's why I was so surprised when Laura came to me that day.

"Hello, I'm Laura. Are you from India?" she asked.

"Hi Laura, I am Pooja... And yes, I am from India." I replied.

"Pooja, if you have time, I would love to talk to you."

"Yes, I would like it too," I said outwardly, but a thought crossed my mind.

'Why would she want to communicate with an ordinary girl like me?'

When we met on the weekend, I came to know why she wanted to meet me. She was going to write a thesis on Ancient Indian Temples for her Doctorate. It would include information about Indian culture and she wondered if I could help her in any way. I readily agreed to help since I had some knowledge about Indian culture, temples, etc. due to the influence of my religious grandparents, my education in a Marathi medium school, and visits to many temples with my parents. But eventually, I realized how limited and superfluous my knowledge was- and on the contrary, how deep her study of Indian culture was. Though I couldn't be of much help to her in her thesis, a link of friendship developed between us. I respected her for her vast knowledge, and I think she liked my simple, straight-forward nature.

Although Denton was a nice city, I decided to look for a job in some other city during the first semester break. Luckily, I got a job for three months at a beachside hotel in a famous tourist town of California.

The first two weeks were spent learning the job, as the tourist season had not yet begun. As I was busy with my work, and Laura with her thesis, we chatted on the phone whenever possible. Once I casually said, "Larua, if you're done with the thesis work, come here for a change and spend a few days with me .... You can meet your sister, too. You said she lives in Morgan Hill, didn't you? It's very close to this place."

"That's a great idea Pooja, I'll come." Laura accepted my invitation and arrived the following week. We were very happy to meet each other. I took three days off from my work and used that time to visit the tourist places nearby like Monterey Bay Aquarium, Seal Sanctuary, Fish Salting Factory, Hall of Mystic Mirrors, etc. One such day, we went to Lovers Point. It was a small beach along the seacoast. At a much higher level, there was a road along the coast line. We hired a tandem cycle and rode the bike -chatting and watching other tourists.

And that's when we saw them. A young man and a donkey foal walking with him. A rope was tied around the foal's neck. But the foal walked so obediently with the young man, that there was no need for a rope! When we got closer, I saw a picture of the foal tattooed on the young man's neck. I was so amused, that I got off the tandem cycle and approached him. I walked a few steps with them and then hesitantly introduced myself. "Hi, I'm Pooja. We don't know each other nor have we met before, but I thought of saying hello to you... because your foal is so cute... and walks with you like a well- behaved kid... I got curious..."

He smiled and then said, "No problem. It happens all the time. I am Mike."

Immediately I asked the next question. "What's the name of your foal?"

Looking at the little one lovingly, he said, "Millie, say hello to Pooja."

Millie turned her head to look at me with her lovely eyes and fluttered the long eye-lashes. She was so cute! I ran my hand over Millie's back, said hi to her, chit-chatted with Mike, walked with them for some distance, then said goodbye to Millie and Mike and returned to the cycle.

"Pooja, come on, what were you talking to them for so long?" Laura asked just one question, and for the rest of the ride, I kept on talking about Millie and Mike.

Laura loved the beach town so much that she extended her stay. As the tourist season started, my working hours increased and I couldn't find time to go for walks with Laura. But she didn't mind. She worked on her thesis in the mornings and walked on the beach in the evenings.

The tourist season slowly came to an end and the day of my return to Denton neared. Laura said she would like to stay back, saying her thesis work could be done from there as well. So, I took a one-day break from my work and went to the beach with her - like the good old days. We met Millie and Mike there. All four of us walked together as if we knew each other for a long time. I walked with Millie and Laura walked with Mike. Laura- whom I knew- was always a serious girl, but now she had become very cheerful, I noticed. "The air of the sea seems to suit you!" I teased her. She just smiled in response.

Laura, who had come for one week break, continued to stay there for the next few months- even after I returned to Denton.

Laura

When I saw Mike that day, I felt he was different than the other men whom I had met before, though I couldn't pinpoint the difference. So, I extended my stay in the beach town so that I would get to know him better. Mike was a soft spoken, unassuming young man. He had studied at Stanford University and still, preferred to live in that beach town to any other big City. His family's farm was at some distance from there. His father used to manage the farm. Also, they had an art store in the nearby Artist Village which he managed in the mornings. The works of art made by the village artists were displayed and sold in that shop. In the evenings his mother Linda would take care of the shop and Mike would take Millie for a walk. Then I started going for a walk with both of them every evening. I started liking him. During our walks, I thought we'd talk about us, but Mike talked mostly to Millie or about Millie.

One day I suggested, " Mike, tomorrow -shall we- I mean, - only the two of us go out somewhere?"

He said, "Come on Laura, it's just the two of us every day, isn't it...?"

"But Millie is with us every day," I said in a slightly disappointed tone.

"She'll always be with us, what's the problem?" he asked in surprise.

Didn't Mike know TWO IS COMPANY, THREE IS CROWD? -Even if the third one is a foal...

Linda

For the past few weeks, I had heard a name -Laura –popping up several times in Mike's conversation. I got curious. So, I told him that someday, I would like to meet Laura; so on that day Mike had invited his girlfriend to our farmhouse.

She wasn't as slim as the typical girls these days, but she looked pretty. We sat on the backyard deck and chatted a lot. She was intelligent and I liked her versatility. While talking, she asked the question I was expecting. "Mike likes Millie a lot, doesn't he?"

"Yes, he does ..., she's been raised on our farm ever since she was born. Mike had been taking care of her since then. He feeds her, bathes her, cuts her hair, takes her for walks, in fact Millie is inseparable from him..." I replied.

"... But, what about his girlfriend? Doesn't she mind?" Laura asked.

I was in two minds, whether to reveal the truth to Laura or not... I was lost in that painful memory.

"Laura, ... Mike's girlfriend – Mildred - is no longer in this world. They were engaged... but a month before the wedding, Mildred passed away in an unfortunate accident. Mike was totally devastated... We didn't know how to get him out of that sorrow. His friends also tried to cheer him up... months passed by... but nothing helped... Once, I heard one of his Indian friends telling him, "... In Hindu religion, we believe that; not only the human body but everything that we see is made of *Panch Tattvas* - the five basic elements, and everything is perishable... Even if a human body is dead and gone, the soul is immortal ... it is born again in some other form... 'etc. Mike listened intently, reflected over the new thought and slowly calmed down... But after that a new problem started."

Remembering those difficult days made me sad.

"Mike came to know that, on the tenth day of Mildred's death, a donkey-foal was born on our farm. So, Mike believed that the new-born foal was the reincarnation of Mildred and he named her Millie. I tried to convince him that there was no such thing as reincarnation, but he persisted... All this happened about a year ago. I don't think too much about it now, because Mike became calmer since the time Millie came into his life."

After a pause, I asked her, "Laura, Mike had mentioned that you have studied Indian culture. So, tell me, is that sort of reincarnation really possible?"

Laura was in deep thought. "Who knows...!" she said aloud. "Honestly, Linda, my research is mostly about the ancient Indian temples and the cultural aspect that goes with it. So far, I haven't come across anything about reincarnation in my studies ..."

I liked her honesty. As a reminder of this visit, I gave her a small gift and an invitation to come again.

Laura

I liked Linda. How understanding and loving she was. Just like Mike.

The next week, when Mike, Millie, and I went for a walk on the beach as usual, Mike suddenly knelt in front of me on the sands of Lovers Point. "Laura, I love you... Will you marry me?" he asked in an emotional voice.

Just as I was about to say yes, I saw Millie looking at me in the eye... and I said, "Will you give me some time to think?"

"Oh Laura, I'll definitely wait until the end of the world, but please say 'yes' " he pleaded, and lovingly wrapped his arms around my waist. I also laughed and changed the topic. I knew that I loved Mike, then why couldn't I say yes to him right away?

... Because, from the day I met Linda, there was a storm of thoughts in my head. Could Millie really be Mildred? ... Is that why Mike is so obsessed with Millie? ... If I say yes to Mike, would Millie be Mike's first love - forever? ... Would I be side-lined? ...Would I have to play the second fiddle?... Can I live my entire life with... Ohhh..., I felt as if my head was spinning..., I couldn't come to a conclusion.

Then I called and told my mom everything about Mike and Millie. She told me to grow up, make my own decisions and take responsibility for it. My father said that in our religion there was no such thing as reincarnation so I should not worry about Millie. My sister told me to be straightforward with Mike and refuse his proposal. There is no need for Mike or Millie - she told bluntly.

Three contradictory opinions...! A tangle of thoughts again. To solve it, as a last hope, I called Pooja and told her everything. She was very happy to know about Mike and I- loving each other. Then I asked Pooja the question about reincarnation that Linda had asked me.

Pooja answered in her typical straight forward way.

"Laura, it is true that our religion believes in reincarnation. But it cannot be predicted as to where, when, how and in which life form that birth will be... What's more, even the new-born soul has no memory of the previous life..." after a brief pause, she continued, "For the time being, let's accept what Mike believes - that Millie is Mildred... Whether his belief is right or wrong can't be tested or proved - but it's this very belief - that pulled him out of his shattered condition after Mildred's death..." Pooja spoke from her heart. "The truth is, even if, let's say...Millie is Mildred, she can't become 'life partner' of Mike. Isn't It?" Very earnestly Pooja tried to convince me more and more.

But I continued my rant, "Even if I agree with you, I know Mike won't separate from her... I can't digest the thought of living with that Millie in my house forever..." I was upset... with myself - and Pooja also... so I blurted out, "Pooja, if you care so much for him, ... why don't you marry him?... I don't mind..."

"Yes, I would have... but he is in love with you..." Pooja said angrily and hung up the phone. I was disturbed by the thought that Pooja, who was always cool, got so angry. After staying up all night, reconsidering everything, I made a decision.

^^^^^^^^^^^^^^^^^

Laura

Pooja applied for a week's holiday from college and came to the beach town from Denton. Mike and Millie were as delighted as I was after meeting Pooja.

My parents, other family members, friends also came for our wedding. We bowed before the Priest and Jesus in the church, exchanged rings and took the oath to support each other throughout our lives. Holding my wedding gown and flower bouquet with my left hand and Mike's reassuring hand with my right hand, I stepped out of the church to the sound of applause.

On the first step of the church, Mike stopped. I knew his eyes were searching for Millie. Recognizing it, Linda, who stood just behind us, came forward and said,

"Mike, Millie will stay with us from now on." Linda said.

"But Mom, you..." His father stopped Mike and said, "She'll stay at our farm. Next year, we will find a suitable mate for her. Don't worry about her at all. Laura and you start a new life... Be happy, God Bless You... "

"Thank you so much...," said Mike. To my great surprise, he agreed without any hesitation... Beaming with joy, I too went towards the parking lot with Mike and both of us hugged Millie. Mike promised Millie that he would see her after returning from our honeymoon. He waved goodbye lovingly and took me by the hand to his car decorated with orchids and a 'Just Married' board.

Before sitting in the car, I tossed the bouquet over my shoulder. It fell in Pooja's hands. We both looked at each other and smiled. Through that smile, we shared a secret... that only two of us knew.

After brainstorming that night, I had understood what Pooja meant. She had said,

"The truth is, even if Millie is Mildred, she can't be Mike's life partner... Just imagine, If Mike loves Millie - the donkey foal - so much, how much will he love you? ... Where will you find another man like that?... "

What she said was so true...

Mike was such a gem of a man... Had I rejected him, I would have been the most foolish, most stupid girl, ... a 'doctor' having a lesser IQ than Millie- the donkey...

* * * * * * * * * * * * * * * * * * * *

* * * * * * * * * * * * *

III
Allergy

Slowly, I was gaining consciousness. Through my partially opened eyes, I could make out my mother-in-law fanning me, my newly wedded husband sprinkling water on my face, my co-sister massaging the soles of my feet, and my father-in-law urgently summoning the doctor...

I looked at them blankly... without my knowledge, I slipped into unconsciousness once again and slowly, my life of the past 20 years flashed before my eyes.

∧∧∧∧∧∧∧∧

That day I got thirsty while playing, so I came home. Outside the door I noticed somebody's *chappals*. Some aunt must be visiting mother. *Oh, if she sees me, at least 15 minutes of my play time would be wasted...* I thought. To avoid answering her queries, I hurriedly opened the door and shouted across the room, "Mom, I am going out to play with Kamali..."

Though I hid behind the kitchen wall and slowly sipped the water, my ears were focused towards the kitchen. I was curious to know who the new aunt was because her voice sounded unfamiliar...

Even though I was not visible from the kitchen, I wondered how my mother knew that I was there. "Hey Vasu, come in. Look who has come..." she called. I had to go inside.

"This is Namu aunty, my friend." Mother introduced me to the aunty. I immediately greeted her with a *Namaskar*.

I always behaved very politely in front of the guests and spoke to them in soft tones. So, as usual, the guest aunty was very much impressed.

"Kalindi, your daughter is so sweet and well behaved ..." Namu aunty commented smiling at me and asked softly, "So... Vasu, would you like to join our school from June?".

Reluctantly, I nodded my head and announced that "Kamli will be waiting for me" and ran away.

"Shssss, I don't want to go to school... So what if Padmatai goes, let her go." I vehemently told Kamali; but mother and father thwarted my resolve and in June, I joined Narmadabai Thatte's

(Namu aunt's) school- 'Balvikas Mandir.'

∧∧∧∧∧∧∧∧∧

Ours was the first batch. The school had only two rooms and two teachers. In one room was *Bigri* class (LKG) and the other room was the Office. *Bigri* class had only 12 students- 8 boys and 4 girls...Thatte Bai- (mother had warned me to call Namu aunty as "Bai" in school-) used to teach us numbers, shlokas, Mararthi *Barakhdi* (script) etc. and Thakar Bai used to teach us games, songs, skits etc. Sports and dance were two of my most favourite subjects. Of course, Thakar Bai was my favourite teacher. Surprisingly, I started liking the school. Going to school was fun- till the third grade. It was from there that the difficult period of my life began.

Our neighbour's daughter- Saudamini- was studying in "Adarsh Vidya Kendra". She had appeared for the Jagannath Shankarshet Scholarship in fourth grade and she had got it also... It was very prestigious to get that scholarship. It seems, my elder sister Padmatai had tried, but failed to get it, so my mother had resolved that I must succeed in getting that scholarship and so she decided to enrol me in Saudamini's school. "I don't want to go to a new school." I resisted, threw tantrums, but all in vain...

Even my father tried to convince my mother, but she told him, "Let Vasu go to Saudamini's school. There, she will learn to work hard and learn some discipline. I am sure she will get the Shankarshet Scholarship... but if not, at least she would become a 'Su-gruhini' (adorable housewife) when she grows up - like Shalu..."

Shaluakka was my eldest sister. I knew that she was married, but I didn't know what is meant by 'Su-gruhini'...

∧∧∧∧∧∧∧∧∧

The new school was very big and there were only girls in that school. There were so many classrooms and so many subjects to study... a different teacher to teach a different subject... Unlike my earlier school, in the new school, discipline and system were most important. Every morning, everybody assembled in a big hall. Only after reciting prayers, we went to class- silently and strictly in a single line. If someone came out of line, the P. T. Master caned her.

Within two days, I developed a total aversion to the new school.

Then that dreadful day arrived. My first Wednesday at the new school.

The teacher for the fourth period entered the classroom and there was silence everywhere.

"Namaste teacher." The girls said in unison.

"Namaste students. Sit down."

We sat down. "Do you remember what you learnt last year?" asked the teacher. "Yessss" everyone shouted in chorus.

"Good... so, take out the class material. This year, you will learn how to cut necks..." she said.

Cutting necks... Oh my god... I was so afraid to look at the demon teacher that I put my head on the desk...

"Madam, she is crying. " my neighbour girl promptly reported to the teacher.

"Why... what happened...?" The teacher came near me and lifted my head.

"Oh... Are you new to this school? I don't remember seeing you last year... What is your name...?" she asked kindly.

I wiped the tears in my eyes and answered, "My name is Vasudha Shankar Lele. I have come to this school from Balvikas Mandir." I answered in complete sentences as taught by my father.

"Eesh... Which school is that?" The girl in the seat behind me whispered and some of them giggled as though they were tickled.

"Keep quiet girls..." the teacher warned them and asked me, "So, tell me Vasudha, why are you crying?"

"Because I am afraid of blood." I replied.

"Blood?" the teacher looked confused. So, I explained. "Last year when my finger got cut, so much blood came... when I cut necks, so much more blood would pour out... I don't want to cut any necks..." I blurted out, sobbing again.

Now the whole class started laughing, including the teacher. But then she said, "Oh Vasudha... There will not be any blood. Don't worry... I teach how to cut necklines of dresses. This is a tailoring class. Didn't you know?"

I stopped crying at once and looked around me sheepishly. All eyes were focused on me and everybody looked amused – at my cost...

I had to start tailoring lessons from the beginning. Since I didn't have any tailoring material, the teacher gave me a piece of cloth, needle and thread. Then she taught me how to thread a needle. I tried hard. That period was spent trying to figure out how the needle could be threaded. Turn by turn, I held the needle in each hand and the thread in the other hand, but couldn't figure out how to thread it... However, by the end of the period, my eyes got a squint by trying to focus on the needle eye...

At last, I succeeded in threading the needle. The next two months I was stuck with a variety of stitches. I wondered how nobody had noticed that the names didn't match the stitches. Running stitch didn't run, hemming stitch wasn't discovered by Hema, cross stitch looked like "x", French knot was just a series of dots and so on... whatever the names, I had to learn all those stitches. I did not dare ask these questions to the teacher. Just continued to stitch as best as I could. My progress was very slow. By the time I reached 'basic neck cutting', the rest of my class had mastered cutting half a dozen shapes of necklines.

Not only did I miss Shankarshet scholarship in 4th grade but I was ranked 13th or 14th in the annual exam, because despite getting good marks in all other subjects, I barely passed in sewing.

When my mother questioned my poor marks in sewing, I simply said, "The teacher is biased. In the exam, they asked us to sew worm stitches. That Maithili Gadgil stitched a rose flower with worm stitches, she gave her full marks. And looking at my stitches, teacher said, "They look like worms in rice, isn't it Vasudha?"... That means, my stitches were real worm stitches, isn't it? But the teacher gave me low marks, isn't this partiality?" I was angry and crying at the same time.

Seeing the tears in my eyes, mom said, "Well, so be it, score good marks next year Vasu.".

I had decided to study 'drawing' from the fifth grade. In my opinion, drawing was an 'easy-to-pass' subject. If you draw a triangle - it's a mountain, triangle placed on a rectangle is a house, half round is sun, only lines are sunrays, amoeba is for tree and wavy lines are for a river... so simple...

My mother approved the change of subject, but it was not possible. As the drawing section was already filled, I had to continue sewing in 5th, 6th, 7th and 8th grades.

As I progressed to higher grades, I got more doubts and questions in my mind about sewing. Tailoring teacher Vaidyabai and I suffered a lot in those years.

I had realised to my great horror that, not only necklines but every part of a dress has innumerable options...why?... And even if they are there, why should we learn those?

Am I going to be a seamstress instead of being a doctor, engineer, or at least a '*Su-gruhini*?...

I struggled to keep pace with the class, but in vain. Anyway I had to stitch handkerchief, baby cap, jabla, slip, nappy, bib, baby frock, blanket, swaddle, shirt....

During those four years, I sewed various types of collars till my neck became stiff...

I sewed balloon, ruffled, flowy, pleated, sleeveless sleeves despite pain in the shoulders...

I got exhausted while sewing the pockets. Pocket for frock, shirt, hidden in the side seam, visible in the front, a secret pocket...

I remember, there was a cloth shop in front of our school gate. A board was placed on the shop-door which read, "Beware of pickpockets."

I was so disgusted with the pocket types that under that board, I stuck a new note.

"However, if the pockets are cut, they will be sewed up at 7-B, Adarsh Vidya Kendra, Girls' School."

Everybody could guess who could have written such an outrageous note but there was no evidence!!! ... So, the next day my whole class (7-B) was punished by the headmistress.

After I passed 8th standard, the Tailoring teacher came to our house and gave me a big hug and a big Cadbury chocolate ... to celebrate my exit from her tailoring class...!

Those five years, fourth to eighth, my report card looked like a beautiful silk dress- with a patch of hessian cloth stitched on it...

'Sewing' class ended in the 9th grade. I passed SSC with seven subjects- two maths, two sciences and three languages. I was ranked second in the school, bagged 96 out of 100 marks in maths, and in the next four years became an engineer without a hitch.

∧∧∧∧∧∧∧∧∧∧∧∧∧∧∧∧∧∧∧∧∧∧∧

A new phase in my life began. There were some changes in our family also during that time. Silver strands appeared in mother's hair, father retired, Padmatai got married and Shalu Akka got a son. Sending of my CV for getting a job and prospective groom search started. One day when I returned from the job interview, mother said, "Vasu, get ready soon, they are coming to *see* you."

Five or six people came home that evening - a handsome young man, his parents, his brother with wife and their little daughter.

Carrying a tray of *Poha* and Tea, I entered the room with Padmatai. I served *Poha* to everyone and stood patiently. When Padmatai signalled me, I sat down at the corner of a sofa chair.

I always behaved very politely in front of guests and spoke in soft tones. I answered all the questions they asked in complete sentences.

The last question was asked by the senior lady in the group. "In which school did you study, Vasudha?"

"I studied in 'Balvikas Mandir' from KG-1 to 3rd standard and from 4th to 11th standard I studied in 'Adarsh Vidya Kendra, Girls school."

"Wow, great." She exclaimed.

That day, I was not successful in the job interview but was selected in this interview. On an auspicious day, I crossed the threshold of the in-laws' house, becoming 'Vasudha Vinayak Gokhale'. My mother-in-law welcomed us with *arti* and the relatives gathered in the house showered flowers on us. Then my mother-in-law took me to the pooja room in the house, applied *Kumkum* on my forehead, gave me milk and banana and placed a beautiful engraved silver box in my hand.

"Vasudha, this is a special gift for you from me... because you are going to be my heir." I was overwhelmed with joy when I heard that...

After going to our room, I eagerly opened the box given by my mother-in-law. There was a key in it. *On the very first day, mother-in-law has trusted me with the locker key... it's a big responsibility, I must prove myself worth that trust...'* I felt nervous.

"Vasudha, keep that key in the box, ...let's find the key to our happy life" said Vinayak switching off the lights.

Next day my niece – Anagha – showed me every room in our two-story house with a running commentary. Finally, we went to the terrace. There were several flowering plants along the parapet wall and adjacent to the staircase was a small room. "What is this room for?" I asked.

"I don't know, it's always closed." She pursed her lips.

"*Chachi*, look at that rose! Every day I water the garden", she said proudly.

"Oh wow, your garden is so beautiful," I said, appreciating her.

On the third day, we were busy with the Satyanarayana pooja. Though my mother-in-law suffered from chronic knee-pain, she took me to the terrace in the evening. "Here is my special gift for you," she said, opening the door of the room with a key from a bunch of keys tied to her waist.

Seeing that gift, my head started spinning. Her voice was ringing in my ears.

"You know Vasudha, when you told me that you were an Adarsh Vidya Kendra student, I knew that only you could be my heir... so for you, I bought a brand new and the latest model in the market... By the way, that old one is mine... I told Vinayak...'" She continued speaking but I could hardly hear her voice... I was so feeble... I was drifting into unconsciousness...

I don't know how long I was like that but when I was regaining consciousness, I could make out my mother-in-law fanning me, my recently wedded husband gently splashing water on my face, my co-sister massaging the soles of my feet, and my father-in-law urgently summoning the doctor. But – I had passed out again.

∧∧∧∧∧∧∧∧∧∧∧∧∧

When I became fully conscious, I saw that my mother was sitting beside my mother-in-law in the terrace room.

"How did Vasudha become unconscious like this?... I was so worried, Kalindibai... that's why I called you." There was deep concern in my mother-in-law's voice.

"There's nothing to worry about, Nalinibai. It's just because of some allergy. I am very sorry... I should have told you before, but I forgot..." My mother said apologetically.

"Oh... is it? What kind of allergy?" asked my mother-in-law.

Looking at the new 'Singer Fashion-Maker' in the room, my mother confided to my mother-in-law in a low voice.

"Vasudha has a terrible allergy to sewing, what to do..."

* * * * * * * * * * * * * * * *

* * * * * * * * * * * * * *

IV
Nominee

"Your call," Shantaram handed over the mobile to Geeta as she came out of the bathroom.

"Whose is it?"

"Suma's"

Geeta took the phone and then they chatted for a long time. They were happy to exchange notes about themselves and their families. Concluding their conversation Geeta said,

"Suma, I am so glad that you called... It's been ages since we spoke to each other..."

"True, it was really nice to pick up the threads after so many years... Actually, I wanted to share some good news with you... we have relocated from Pune to Mysore. Now we can meet again. And can you believe it! we've got a house in the same layout where you used to live!"

"Is it? But how do you know where we lived?" Geeta exclaimed.

"It's an interesting story. On the third day of our shifting to Mysore, a maid came looking for work. I asked her for some references. To my great surprise, one of the references was yours. In fact, I got your number from her. When I asked further, she said that she worked with you for 5 years and that your family had left for Bangalore. So, besides catching up with you, this was one more reason why I called you. – Is she good? Should I employ her?" Suma asked.

"You must be talking about Jaya." Said Geetha with a smile on her face. "You need not worry Suma; she is very honest and sincere." Geeta vouched for Jaya.

Geeta kept thinking about Jaya, even after the call ended.

^^^^^^^^^^^^

That year, Geeta's husband - Shantaram was transferred from Davangere to Mysore. After unloading luggage at the bungalow, the truck had returned.

They had shifted houses many times but every time, Geeta used to get a little tense until all the stuff was put in place. While thinking about which box to open first, someone peeped in through the open door.

"Namaste Akka, I'm Jaya, I work in the opposite bungalow. I saw the transport truck returning from your house, so, just came to ask; do you need a maid?" She asked with a smile on her face.

Geeta didn't know what to say. She had not expected a woman to just walk in and ask for work... she seems to be overconfident, Geeta thought.

"What do you think? Should I say yes?" Geeta asked Shantaram in Marathi.

"Anyway, you need a maid... And if you have any doubts; you can crosscheck her credibility from the opposite house. I think you can employ her." Shantaram said. When asked how much salary she expected, Jaya said that she would be happy to get the same amount as the lady in the opposite bungalow paid her.

So, Jaya was employed. She was of great help to Geeta in unpacking the boxes and organizing the household items.

Jaya would chit-chat while having her tea and breakfast that Geeta gave her after she finished her daily work, often talking about her family. Hers was a love marriage. Her husband Murali, was working as a peon in some bank. He was not highly educated, but smart. They had two daughters born three years apart. When Jaya did housework, they both played in the garden. Neat, clean, and sincere Jaya soon became a part of Geeta's family. Even if there was some extra work, Jaya did it without complaining. Her speed of work was amazing. Moreover, the work was done so well that Geeta was not given a chance to find any fault.

A year later, when Geeta gave her a raise, Jaya pleaded with her, "Akka, keep that extra money with you. That way, at least some amount would be saved. If I have it, it would be spent on some unnecessary purchases." Geeta appreciated it. Handing over a box with lock and key Geeta said, "Keep your money in it. Think of this box as your locker in the bank."

^ ^ ^ ^ ^ ^ ^ ^ ^ ^ ^ ^

Everything was going smoothly for two-three years. But one day, Jaya- who always came on time- did not come. When she came the next day, Geeta was shocked to see her swollen face and one black eye -

"Oh Jaya, what happened?" Geeta was worried.

"... Akka, I don't know how to explain my plight," she said with a sigh. A few minutes later, she asked,

"Akka, - will you talk to my Murli... Just once?"

"Me? - And what should I talk about to Murali?" Geeta asked in surprise.

"He says he wants a son. For the past three years, I had been dodging his demand for a son, but now he is adamant..."

"But you have two beautiful daughters, isn't that enough?"

"That is what I have been telling him. But he is not willing to listen." Jaya said in a hurt tone.

"Then why don't you ask your mother-in-law to convince him," suggested Geeta.

"Akka, - Last month when I went to the village-fair, I talked to my in-laws about everything. My mother-in-law said, 'Jaya, don't you know that after five girl children, my sixth child was Murali? You have only two daughters. You can take a chance... What's wrong if he wants a son as *Kuladeepak* to carry forward our family name?" I was very angry with my mother-in-law, so I replied to her, "Amma, do you have any ancestral property or a big bank balance to pass on to a '*Kuladeepak*'? ... as far as we are concerned, we live with meager income; we can't afford to have a third child. Besides, during the second delivery, I had an operation to prevent having more children." Hearing this, my mother-in-law got wild and she provoked Murli to get married again."

"Akka, you please talk to him, he will listen if you tell him."Pleaded Jaya.

"Why will he listen to me? In any case, I am a stranger. I have no right to interfere in your personal matters," said Geeta.

"How can you say that Akka, you have only one daughter, no son - and still you are so happy. I know you are the President of some club, and you speak on such issues...Please Akka, for my sake..." Jaya requested so earnestly that Geeta had to agree.

^ ^ ^ ^ ^ ^ ^ ^ ^ ^ ^ ^ ^ ^ ^ ^ ^ ^ ^ ^

The following Sunday, Murli arrived. In as diplomatic a language as she could muster, Geeta told him "The times have changed Murli.

Even a daughter brings honour to family, she is a *'Kuladeepika'*... she also carries forward family name, etcetera." Murli listened everything calmly, and answered,

"Ma'am, you listen to me now. Ours was a love marriage. Initially my mother had not accepted our wedding because Jaya is from a different caste, but I stood my ground. However, after our marriage, she welcomed Jaya wholeheartedly into our family. Yes, my parents are poor, but why should Jaya taunt them about not having ancestral property or bank balance? Isn't it very insulting?"

He continued angrily, "Besides that, Jaya never told me that she had undergone a family planning operation... Without my permission, how could she do that? My head has been spinning ever since I heard it... now that she can't give me a son, Jaya tells me to raise her sister's son like our son," Murli's voice was slowly cracking. "Tell me madam, why should I accept this? I want my own son." After a few minutes, he calmed down and said, "I will take your leave madam. You please advise Jaya to sign the divorce papers."

Geeta couldn't say anything further to convince him because it was clear that Murli would not heed to her advice.

Jaya continued to work but her usual enthusiasm had vanished. Her sad and disheartened expression troubled Geeta. So, a couple of days later Geeta opened the topic with her. "Jaya, I spoke to Murli the other day and tried to convince him but he seems to be hell-bent on divorce..." With great hesitation Geeta continued, "I know, it will be hard for you to be alone, but how long are you going to suffer like this? Divorce seems to be the only option... "

"Akka, you can't imagine how difficult life is for a woman left by her husband... If I agree to divorce, he will force me to vacate the house... Where shall I go with the two daughters? What about household expenses? I don't know whether that evil woman - Sarsu - will let him give me anything at all..."

Geeta was shocked. "Now who is this Sarsu?" she asked.

"She is that watchman's wife who works in the building opposite Murli's bank. Anyway, I made it very clear to Murli that I will not give him a divorce. He can stay with whomever he wants, but if he forces me to leave the house, I will report it to the police... He doesn't come home anymore. lives with her."

"But what about Sarsu's husband? How does he tolerate all this?" Geeta asked.

"That watchman is too old... and stupid and ***..." said Jaya scornfully.

Geeta wanted to help Jaya, but didn't have any immediate solution. Moreover, she was very busy with the Silver Jubilee Celebration of her Club. On that occasion, her Club had taken up a service project- to give vocational training to 25 needy women. For that, talks were going on with a Government Technical Institute that conducted short term tailoring courses. Two hours of class and one hour of practice. Her Club was going to pay the fees for the three months course. Geeta sponsored fees for three women trainees. Jaya was one of them.

At the end of the course, on Dussehra day, Diploma certificates were to be given to the successful trainees. But Geeta could not attend that ceremony. Before that itself, Geeta had to go to Bangalore along with her daughter- who had got a seat in Bangalore Medical College.

While packing the luggage with the help of Jaya, Geeta remembered how she had helped in unpacking their luggage five years back... Their eyes were filled with tears. Before leaving, Geeta handed over Jaya's 'locker' to her, and also gave some additional money.

After Dussehra, Geeta's Club President called her to inform that the Silver Jubilee Project was successful. All the women had completed their tailoring diploma course and Jaya had got second rank in her class.

Of course, Geeta was very happy with that news.

^^^^^^^^^^^^^^^^^^^

Shantaram occasionally went to Mysore for work, but it used to be a daytrip. This time, he was going to stay in Mysore, so Geeta also accompanied him. While he was busy attending the conference, Geeta went to meet Suma at her house. After the delicious lunch they were chatting leisurely.

"Didn't Jaya come today?" Geeta enquired.

"She quit."

"Oh, ... but why?" Geeta asked in surprise.

"She said she was going to live elsewhere, so she would not be able to come to work."

"But didn't she have her own house in Kanaknagar- on the other side of this layout?"

"Yes, but she sold it." Suma said.

"I thought I would meet her at your house." Suma felt the disappointment in Geeta's voice.

"I have her number. I'll call her and tell that you are here." said Suma.

^^^^^^^^^^

The next day, Jaya went to meet Geeta at her hotel.

"Akka, my little gift..." Jaya said affectionately and handed over a neatly wrapped package to Geeta.

Looking at the silk gown in the package, Geeta exclaimed, "What is the need to give me such an expensive gift?"

"Akka, I have stitched this gown," Jaya said proudly.

"Oh wow, then I must wear it," Geeta said heartily. She enquired about Jaya's daughters and then asked casually, "Suma was saying that you are not living in Kanaknagar anymore... How come you decided to sell that house? For that house... you even left Murli." Geeta had finally asked the question that was bothering her.

After some hesitation Jaya spoke. "Akka, Murli had gone to live with that other woman – Sarsu, remember?"

"Yes, I remember," Geeta said.

"After that, he stopped giving me money. It became very difficult for me to run my family. Somehow, I managed by working in three more houses to meet my monthly expenses. But due to that strain, I started getting back pain. At that time, my daughters helped me. They are gems, they never insisted on anything. We were going through a tough time. That hardship continued for two-and-a-half years."

She was deeply moved by the troublesome memories.

"Then one day a man from Murli's bank came looking for me." She continued. He said that the bank manager had called me. I went. Manager gave me horrible news. He told me that three weeks back, Murli's cycle was hit by a truck and he died on the spot. It was such a shock for me...Suddenly my mouth went dry... My hands and feet went cold... I didn't know how to respond ...Then he also told me that a woman by name Sarasu- had come to claim Murli's pension; so, he checked the papers. After our marriage, Murli had written my name as 'NOMINEE' and it was still there. That's why the manager had sent a message to me to meet him" Jaya explained.

"After giving all the required documents I started getting Murli's pension. As his 'Nominee', the house also was transferred in my name. But after his death, I was not comfortable living there, so I sold the house and moved elsewhere."

Jaya was reliving those days. "Akka, I didn't want Murli's money. I wanted him..." She sighed and continued, "I made a fixed deposit of the house sale money, it will be useful for the marriage of our daughters. His pension- I use for our daughters' education. For my household expenses I earn myself. Few moments of silence and then she continued, "Akka, I took that tailoring course only because you told me to, but if it hadn't been for that, I would still be washing dishes in other people's houses."

"After moving to a different locality, I spent the money from the locker you gave me to buy a sewing machine and I started a tailoring business. Now, I have employed two women to help me cope with the work. Everything is going well for us now. All thanks to you Akka," Jaya expressed her gratitude with a namaskar.

"Jaya, I'm really happy for you," Geeta said joyfully. But with a sigh Jaya said in a sad voice,

"Just one thought does not leave my mind. Murli ceased to be my 'husband' when he left me and went to her, - that's when our husband-wife relationship ended... However, the law kept it alive - but only - on paper. Akka, ...What's the use of being a NOMINEE after his death - while I was just his *paper wife*... Wife as per documents, when he was alive..." Jaya could not control her tears...

Geeta could understand her pain. She was in deep thought. After a while she said,

"Life is very strange, Jaya. You can never predict what will happen when. It has a lot of twists and turns. At one such turn, Murli held your hand... and later... at one of the twisted turns, he let go of your hand... From then on, you trudged the painful path alone. His untimely, accidental death was also another such turn. Ironically, after that sad turn, your life changed... perhaps, for better..."

"Incidentally, Murli- who made your life miserable when he was alive, has – unintentionally - made your life easier after his accidental death. In fact, I doubt, had he been alive, whether he would have earnestly cared for your daughters..."

After pausing for a moment, Gita continued, "And anyway, for eight or nine years both of you were happily married, you gave him two beautiful daughters... Isn't it? So, you have always been his real wife. Why do you think of yourself as a 'paper wife'? And most importantly, you spend his money for his daughters, their education, their upbringing, isn't it? So, you are not just a NOMINEE, you are the TRUSTEE of his money."

Jaya was listening attentively to Geeta's speech. Her face brightened. With great satisfaction she said,

"Akka, you have given me a new *vision* today - to look at myself. I'm neither a 'paper wife' nor just a 'NOMINEE'-- but I'm a trustee-reliable and responsible- TRUSTEE."

* * * * * * * * * * * * * * * * * *

* * * * * * * * * * * * *

V
Rangoli

Sharayu was fast asleep when the mobile phone on her bedside table began to ring.

She picked it up and answered in a sleepy voice, "Hello."

"Hello... Sharayu?... it's me, Madhav... Sorry for calling at this hour."

Sharayu glanced at the clock. It was well past midnight.

"What happened, Madhav Bhaiya?" her voice was laced with concern.

"Early this morning Dinu Uncle was admitted to a hospital in Bengaluru. He had another stroke."

"How is he now?" Sharayu's voice trembled with worry as she asked.

"...I don't know what to say, Sharayu..."

Sensing the hesitation in Madhav's voice, Sharayu enquired further, "What did the doctors say?"

"Currently, he is under observation in the ICU. Given that this was his second stroke, the doctors said they can't predict anything for the next 24 hours."

"Madhav Bhaiya, will Daddy be alright?" she asked in a choked voice. Madhav could hear her sobbing.

"Sharayu..., please, don't cry..., we're all here. The treatment has started and the doctors are doing their best," Madhav consoled her.

The sound of Sharayu's suppressed sobs woke up Sumant - her husband.

"What happened, Sharu?" he asked, but Sharayu was so sad that she couldn't answer. Wiping the tears in her eyes, she just handed him the mobile. After Madhav explained everything to him, Sumant assured Madhav "Don't worry Madhav, I'll send Sharu to India at the earliest. Everything will be fine..."

Neither Sharayu, nor Sumant could sleep peacefully that night.

Sumant had immense respect for Sharayu's father Dinkar Rao, - not only because he was his father-in-law, but also because he was a fine gentleman. Though Sumant also wished to be with Dinakar Rao in his hour of need and be of help to Sharayu, he had to stay back to complete an urgent submission at his office.

So, Sumant booked Sharayu on the earliest flight available to Bengaluru.

Next morning, Maira - Sharayu's daughter- watched intently as Sharayu packed her suitcase. "Mumma, are you going somewhere?" she asked with tears welling up in her eyes.

"Yes, baby."

"Where?"

"I am going to India. Your grandpa is unwell. I'm going to visit him," Sharayu explained.

"But that is not fair, Mumma... You promised me that you would attend my school function today," seven-year-old Maira grumbled. Sharayu tried hard but couldn't bring herself to negotiate with Maira. Finally, after promising to take her to Disneyland after returning from India, Maira ended her protest.

^^^^^^^^^^^^^^^^^^^^^^^^^

Sharayu boarded the plane. As the flight took off, passengers were greeted by the air hostess, followed by the pilot's announcements about the flight route, altitude etc. Then, as usual, the flight safety instructions were announced and welcome drinks were served. But Sharayu was totally lost in her thoughts, unaware of everything around her.

'Hope Maira is doing fine... It's the first time that she is staying alone with Sumant, without me around... hope Sumant is able to manage her... I myself never wanted to stay away from Mummy and Daddy. Even after marriage, I wanted to live in India, so that I would be available to them for any emergency... but in reality, I am so far away from them... on the other side of the globe... How many times have I met them after my marriage? ... maybe thrice... once in India and twice when they visited us in the USA...' thoughts rushed through her mind at supersonic speed.

It was only when the stewardess asked "Veg or non-veg?" that Sharayu realized that she hadn't paid attention to her meal preference while booking the ticket. "Veg" Sharayu replied. Although Sumant knew that she always preferred vegetarian meals while traveling, this time, amidst the rush of booking tickets, he also must have forgotten to mention her food preference, she thought.

Sharayu was the only child of Dinkar Rao and Rama Bai. At home she was loved and adored by her parents as she was born after many years of their marriage. Even at school she was liked by all the teachers because she was a brilliant and well-behaved student. Sharayu completed schooling with flying colours from the local school. She could have got admission in any college in Bengaluru, but she preferred to study in the nearby college in Mandya so that she could live with her parents. When she was studying in the last year of her degree course, her parents started searching for an alliance for her. Sharayu had only one condition ... that the boy should be working and living in India, so that she could meet her parents whenever she wished to. It so happened that Madhav's friend - Sumant- who had a job in Bengaluru, asked for Sharayu's hand in marriage. Everybody in both the families approved the match. Soon Sharayu and Sumant got married and started their new life in Bengaluru.

Every month, Sharayu used to visit her parents and spend one weekend with them. Her mother used to prepare Sharayu's favorite dishes. Sharayu would meet her friends and would visit local temples. She used to enjoy those visits. But it didn't last for long.

A year after their marriage, Sumant's India office offered him a contract for two years to work in the USA head office. "It's a question of just two years, time will fly, and before you realize, we will be back to India," Sumant had convinced Sharayu when they left for the USA. However, his company kept extending the contract period, and thus for the past nine years, they were living in the USA. Sharayu was overwhelmed with the feeling of guilt... guilt for living so far away for so long from her parents...

"Daddy, next time when you visit us, you must stay here for six months..." Sumant and Sharayu had insisted repeatedly during the last visit of her parents to the USA.

"After I retire from the bank, we will certainly stay for 6 months." Dinkar Rao had promised wholeheartedly. But it wasn't destined to happen...

∧∧∧∧∧∧∧∧∧∧∧∧∧∧∧∧∧∧

When the *fasten your seat belt* sign flashed and an announcement was made, Sharayu snapped out of her daze. Her flight landed at Dubai Airport. The connecting flight was after three hours. As Sharayu sat down with a cup of Starbucks coffee in her hand, she remembered her mother's filter coffee. The aroma of that filter coffee filled her mind. She smiled happily. Once again, she was lost in recollecting her memories. She remembered fondly how everything that her mother did, be it cooking or knitting or drawing rangoli, it used to be very neat and artistic... Even Meera Bai's bhajans sung in her melodious voice were a treat to the ears...

Everybody who met Sharayu, used to say that her parents were made for each other... a perfect match...And that was so true. Both of them were highly talented. But besides that, they also shared a common interest - to serve the needy.

That's why, while working as a Bank Manager, Dinkar Rao had acquired a degree in homeopathy, and in his spare time, he provided free homeopathic treatment and medicines to people in the village. Despite receiving a promotion and a transfer to Bengaluru, he decided to remain at the village branch of his bank. His decision stemmed from his desire to use his knowledge in homeopathy to provide healthcare to the residents of nearby villages and enhance their well-being. People who had benefited from his medicines sang praises of Dinkar Rao. They held a special place for him in their hearts.

'So many patients were cured by him, why couldn't he cure himself?' Sharayu thought sadly.

From the Kempe Gowda International Airport of Bengaluru, Sharayu went straight to the hospital. Seeing the condition of her father from the ICU window, she felt her heart skip a beat. But maintaining a brave face, she assured her mother, "Daddy will soon recover, he will be alright Ma..."

... But on the third day, Dinkar Rao passed away.

Madhav called Sumant and told him everything. After consoling Sharayu over the phone, Sumant said, "Sharu, look, don't worry about us. Stay there with Ma until everything is settled. Take care of her. And yes, when you come, bring her along."

Putting aside the sorrow of losing his beloved younger brother, Sudhakar Rao performed all the rites and rituals himself. One by one, all the relatives left after the thirteenth day ceremony and then Sharayu got an opportunity to speak to her mother in private.

"Ma, Sumant and I feel that instead of staying alone here, please come with me to USA " Sharayu suggested softly.

"No dear, instead of that foreign country, I'd be fine here, in my homeland..." replied Rama Bai.

"But Ma, even if the country is not your homeland, we are there, we are not foreigners... Besides, Maira is there. She'd be so happy to meet you - her grandmother" pleaded Sharayu.

Finally, after a lot of coaxing by Sharayu and Sumant, Rama Bai agreed to go with Sharayu.

Sumant and Maira had come to the airport to receive them. "Maira, look, who has come with Mumma... your grandma..." Sumant drew her attention to Rama Bai.

"Hi" greeted Maira and continued to walk holding Sharayu's hand.

Sharayu didn't like the way Maira greeted her grandmother. But then she justified it to herself with, *"Actually, I shouldn't blame Maira. She hasn't met her grandma before. In fact, she hardly knows her grandma. They had come here only twice, when she was born and again for her third birthday... She knows her grandparents only through my phone conversations with them... and even during those video calls, she just says Hi to them..."* she tried to convince herself and then concluded with *"...today also she did the same... Anyway, I am sure Maira will warm up to her grandma in a couple of weeks..."*

^^^^^^^^^^^^^^^^^^^^

A week had gone by, yet Maira remained distant from her grandmother. She was very angry because she had to share her room with Rama Bai. Her toys' cupboard had been converted into Rama Bai's wardrobe. Her sleep was disturbed as Rama Bai got up very early in the mornings and was awake till late nights. On top of that, she kept repeating something in an unknown language all the time. In short, Maira had lost all her privacy because of 'that grandma'.

Sometimes she had even told her grandmother, "I hate you,"... but said it very softly. Once she complained, "Mumma, my name is Maira, but that lady keeps calling me Meera, Meera...!!! I don't like that name. I don't like her."

"But she likes you as much as I like you. And with great affection she calls you Meera..." replied Sharayu. Maira's yet another complaint was that grandma doesn't understand what Maira tells her. Not that Rama Bai didn't understand English, but it was hard for her to understand Maira's American accent and besides that, she was not conversant with spoken English...

Though Rama Bai could sense and felt sad about Maira's insulting comments, she never expressed her feelings to Sharayu. Whenever Sharyu tried to apologize for Maira's rude behavior, she would tell Sharayu, "She's still young, let it go."

More than three weeks had passed, yet Rama Bai was not getting accustomed to the new place. So, to involve her in the daily chorus, Sharayu started asking Rama Bai's advice about some exclusive recipes. Slowly Rama Bai took over the responsibility of cooking.

Maira was not fond of Indian food in particular, but one of the days Maira had to eat chapati with jam instead of her usual snack of peanut butter-jam sandwich.

"Wow, it's so soft and so yummy!" she exclaimed. And from that day onwards, she became a fan of chapati-jam sandwiches. The smart girl that she was, she had also noticed that her Mumma gets free time to play with her, since the day grandma had started cooking food... After all, there was some benefit of grandma being there, living with them... she realized. Number of her complaints against grandma reduced. Sharayu noticed the change in Maira's behaviour, but still, all was not that well!

∧∧∧∧∧∧∧∧∧∧∧∧∧∧∧

The days and weeks and months passed by and Diwali was soon approaching. Like every year, this year too, Sharayu got a call from her friend Neeta.

"Sharayu, on Sunday, we have a meeting at our house to plan this year's Diwali celebration. As usual, I am inviting both of you to join us and participate actively." she said.

"But Neeta, I'm not in the mood this year," Sharayu replied.

"I can understand Sharayu, but please come. Maybe, meeting friends would elevate your mood..."

Finally, Sharayu went to the meeting. The Kannada community in that part of the city had formed a Kannada Sangha. Sumant and Sharayu were active members in the Sangha. They used to celebrate Indian festivals – not necessarily on the same day of the festival - but on a weekend, as per everybody's convenience. Sharayu got totally involved while discussing Diwali celebration - how, when, where, menu, decorations, etc. She even suggested a novel idea that everybody liked and approved. She returned home in a cheerful mood.

The next morning Sharayu asked Rama Bai "Ma, will you teach me how to make 'Chakli' (an Indian savoury item)?"

"What's there to teach? It's very easy... But where will you get the ingredients?" Rama Bai asked casually.

"We get everything in the Indian store, Ma. Tomorrow we will go there. You also come with me, because I have no knowledge about the ingredients required to make chakli."

That was the first time in the past four months that Rama Bai crossed the compound wall of their house. The next few days Sharayu and Rama Bai spent hours together preparing "Chakli' and "Laddoo'. Maira hovered around them all the while. She certified that grandma's Laddoo tasted better than what they had bought from the Indian Store. She even tried to make Chakli, but when it broke into pieces, she got upset and went to play...

∧∧∧∧∧∧∧∧∧∧∧∧∧∧∧∧

Just three days before the Diwali celebration, Sharayu asked hesitantly, "Ma, all my friends are after me... they want you to draw a "Rangoli..."

"But how do they know that I can draw Rangoli?"

"Actually, I told them..." Sharayu replied sheepishly. "...Please Ma... don't say 'no'.... I have already purchased rangoli powder, colours etc..." Sharayu requested and sincerely hoped that Rama Bai would agree.

Three days later, on Saturday, Rama Bai and Sharayu reached the Diwali Celebration venue, four hours before the program. Sharayu got busy helping the decoration team, and Rama Bai got busy drawing the rangoli. Amidst traditional rangoli design she incorporated the flowers and colourful leaves that she had seen during the fall season in the USA. Overall, the rangoli design as well as colour scheme were very attractive and pleasing to the eyes.

When Sumant and Maira arrived three hours later; they were surprised to see so many people gathered right at the doorstep of the venue. Maira went to see what they were watching. "Wow!!!" she exclaimed. She was delighted to see the beautiful rangoli. Her face lit up just like the *diyas* (Mud lamps) in rangoli. She was thrilled when she could recognize some of the flowers drawn in the rangoli...

Then she began to observe the people around her. Every person who entered the hall - stopped to admire the rangoli. Some of them took photos while some others expressed that they were seeing such a rangoli for the first time. Then she peeped inside the hall. There was a festive atmosphere everywhere. As soon as she entered, she was greeted by her friends. "Happy Diwali" they said and hugged her. Maira felt very happy. Then she spotted her Mumma decorating the tall, shiny brass lamp. A few people were busy with other arrangements and many people were enjoying special Diwali snacks.

She went to the snacks counter. She observed that many ladies were eating Chakli, Ladoo etc. and talking to Rama Bai. Looking at them she thought, *'they seem to be so happy chatting with grandma - in the same language that her Mumma and grandma conversed... What's the name of that language... Hmm, something like...? Yes, it's Canady...'* She picked up a plate with snacks and while munching a piece of Laddoo she continued to think about Rama Bai... *"I think... if all those aunties have surrounded grandma and... and I think, they are praising her ... It means she must be really special... so what if she doesn't drive a car like Kiara's grandma or doesn't wear jeans and T-shirt like Sana's grandma... she must be great in her own way..."* little Maira was lost in her thoughts.

The program began, and everyone watched attentively. After the entertainment program, the Vice President of the Association stood up to propose 'Vote of Thanks'. After thanking everyone who was involved in organizing the celebration, he continued, "All of you would agree with me - that, even though the official welcome for the Diwali Celebration was by Mr. Javali, the President of Kannada Sangha, your true welcome was done by the beautiful rangoli outside the hall. In the cold weather of November, when the general mood is slightly depressing; the bright colors of that beautiful rangoli brought warmth and happiness to each one of us..."

He signaled Sharayu and continued with his speech.

"Ma, let's go, The Vice President is calling you..."

"ME?... Where?... On the stage?... Why?" Rama Bai whispered.

"Yes, come on," and holding her mother's hand, Sharayu walked towards the stage.

"... All of you must be curious to know who drew that captivating rangoli. Let us welcome her to the stage with a standing ovation..."

The whole audience rose happily and clapped loudly as Rama Bai went to the dais.

It was the first time for her to be on the stage. She stood there nervously.

She was embarrassed to receive so much attention and praise...

The Vice President continued;

"... And the artist is - none other than Mrs. Rama Bai Dinakar Rao Huliyar- the mother of Mrs. Sharayu Sumant."

"... And grandmother of Maira... She is MY grandma..." Maira announced proudly from the audience, and all of a sudden, she ran to the stage and hugged Rama Bai tightly.

Rama Bai's face lit up with a happy smile. She felt that Maira's hug was the best reward and appreciation that she had received.

The audience was moved by the scene on the stage. They applauded non-stop.

Rama Bai touched Maira on her head.

Looking up at grandma, Maira smiled lovingly.

And Sharayu?... Her eyes welled with tears of happiness. Her joy knew no boundaries. She wanted to remember... the heart-touching scene of Maira hugging her grandma...

She was amazed to see the transformation in Maira which was brought by the colorful rangoli. The lines in the rangoli design had connected not only the dots... but had connected Rama Bai and Maira too...!

And she was sure that then onwards, the beautiful colors of rangoli design would seep into the relationship of grandmother and the granddaughter...! ...Making it an "Everlasting - Loving - Relationship"!

* * * * * * * * * * * * * * * * * *

* * * * * * * * * * * * *

VI
Barfi (An Indian Sweet)

It had been a month since Mrs. Bharati, my niece and Mr. Vinay Sane, had arrived in Bangalore from Pune. Both were busy on weekdays as they were working in some leading IT Companies and both were newly married (ie, to each other, of course); so I didn't want to disturb the young couple. Besides, our homes were at opposite ends of Bangalore. They lived in White Field – closer to their workplace, and we lived in Vijayanagar. Even if we were to visit them for a short time, it would take one full day - including the travel time. So, we still hadn't met. Instead, we used to talk to each other on the mobile - that too only on weekends.

One day in the afternoon, I received a phone call from her.

"Hello, is this Bharati?" I recognized her voice.

"Yes, Usha *mavashi* (*Mavashi means mother's sister in Marathi*), how are you? Is uncle fine?"

"Yeah, we're fine, but how come you called on a Thursday? Isn't it a working day? Is there any 'good' news?" I asked expectantly...

"Oh ... not the 'good news' that you expect..." she replied shyly. "I called because I want to invite both of you over to our home for lunch. Tomorrow is Good Friday, both of us have a holiday and we will be at home. It's a great opportunity to meet..."

"Tomorrow?... Oh, but not tomorrow..."

"*Mavashi*, I won't accept any excuses... Tell me what time you will come... Come soon, so that we will have enough time to chit-chat."

"Bharati, actually, we have already booked movie tickets for tomorrow. That's the reason I have to decline your invitation, please don't be angry... we can meet some other day..."

I knew that Bharati was obsessed with cinema right from her childhood. So, the next question was expected.

"*Mavashi*, which movie's tickets have you booked?'

"Barfi"

"Oh, wow... it's a Ranbir Kapoor's movie, right?" she exclaimed. "I want to watch it too... Wait a minute, I will call Vinay and ask." She said impatiently.`

After a few moments she said, "Looks like he is in a meeting and is unable to take calls... *Mavashi*, can you book two tickets for us too? We will meet you at the theatre."

"Wow, cool, I like your idea, Bharati... But a small hitch... Our tickets were booked two days back... let me check the availability... and if I get tickets, I'll let you know right away. OK?" I assured.

She was lucky, I got two tickets. I informed her about it and told, "Bharati, please come early to the theatre so that we can have lunch or a quick bite there itself. And after watching the movie, come to our home, have dinner... and then go home on Saturday..."

"Okay," she agreed readily and asked, "Where should we come?"

"Gopalan Mall. Mysore Road,"

"Okay, bye... we will be there, *Mavashi*" she said excitedly and disconnected the phone. I could guess that her boss would have been nearby, so she had hastily cut the call.

The next day, both of us reached Gopalan Mall at 11 o'clock to watch the 12:30 show. Bharati didn't show up, so we spent time window shopping. Around 12 o'clock, she called saying, "Sorry *Mavashi*, looks like we're going to be late. We are caught in a heavy traffic jam. We may not reach on time to have lunch together. So please don't wait for us, you have lunch."

I had skipped breakfast that morning since we were to eat lunch at the mall. It was too late to have proper lunch, so we selected the quickest served items on the menu, shoved it down the stomach, and stood in the queue to enter the theater.

Twenty minutes had passed, still there was no sign of Bharati. So, I called.

"Hey Bharati, where are you? Have you reached?"

"*Mavashi*, we have just reached. We are in the car-parking queue. We will be there in five minutes."

"Oh ok... but we have your tickets..." I said.

"Please ask uncle to send our tickets on WhatsApp. You go in, we will join you..."

"Okay... but come soon"

I agreed, because among the new generation actors, Ranbir Kapoor was my favourite actor; and I didn't want to miss the beginning of his movie.

So, we went in after telling the doorkeeper that two more persons from our group would be coming soon.

^ ^ ^ ^ ^ ^ ^ ^ ^ ^ ^ ^ ^ ^ ^

The doorman closed the doors. The dim lights were put off. It became pitch dark in the theatre... then the screen lit up...advertisements were over... trailers of future films were over ... Jana Gana Mana was played... then titles of the movie were over too.

But Bharati had not come... My mind got distracted from the movie.

"Bharati, where are you guys?" I whispered in my phone, keeping my voice as low as possible.

A few heads turned towards me...

"Hey, we want to watch the movie even if you don't." I was reprimanded by those sitting in front of us.

With a downcast face, I sat restlessly – observing outlines of the latecomers – against the bright screen.

"... Hey, look at her," I pointed at one dark figure moving in the aisle. "Doesn't she look like Bharati... and I think... behind her is Vinay" I whispered again, nudging my husband.

"Yes." He said avoiding the angry gaze of the front row audience.

'At last, they have reached' I muttered to myself and took a deep breath as though my life had come back.

Then onwards, I got totally absorbed in the movie. I was all praise for Ranbir Kapoor and Priyanka Chopra. In my mind, I conferred on them all the awards of the filmy world, including the Oscars (!) for the best actor and actress...

Intermission was over and done with. In those few minutes, one has to get down so many steps and then climb back struggling in the dark. I didn't feel like doing that strenuous exercise. So, I just sat watching the crowd, and sent a message to Bharati, saying 'Let's meet in the food court after the movie'.

The movie ended. We made our way through the crowd and reached the food court. Even after ten minutes of wait, there was no sign of Bharati. Now I was a bit upset. As I was wondering what was going on, why was this girl so late in coming out of the theatre that I got a call. "*Mavashi*, where are you?"

"What do you mean? ... in the food court, waiting for you for so long..." I must have sounded angry.

"Sorry *Mavashi*, but the movie got over just now," she said.

"Ok Ok..." I brushed away her answer and ordered, "come quickly". All of a sudden, I got a bright idea. "Otherwise let's do this, we will wait outside the exit gate of the mall, and you come there directly... Then let's go home and have tea," I suggested my new plan.

It took at least ten minutes for us to come out of the parking maze. We parked our car outside the mall, on the road. The security man told us to move, but we stayed put. "Why is it taking so long for them to come out?" my husband retorted angrily. I had to bear the brunt of his anger silently. I did the only thing that I could. I rang up Bharati.

"Bharati, why are you so much delayed? There's been chaos here on the road. We've been standing outside the gate for the last 15 minutes - just watching the traffic on the flyover... the security man has come twice and has been insisting to leave..." I said in a plaintive tone controlling my agitation.

"*Mavashi*, don't be angry, we also have been waiting for you for a long time... But... wait a minute... what did you say ... watching the traffic on the flyover... Which flyover? ... there's no flyover to be seen here."

"Come on Bharati, how is that possible?"

"Really Mavashi... I don't see any flyover... I can see only the Entrance Arch of Rajarajeshwari Nagar."

My husband was listening to our conversation. "Oh, I know what has happened." Taking the phone from my hand, he said, "Look Bharati, stay where you are. We are coming." Saying this, he started the car. Then he asked me somewhat accusingly, "Had you told them which Gopalan Mall to come to?" I looked at him quizzically. "It's true that all four of us went to see the movie at Gopalan Mall, but there are two Gopalan Malls on Mysore Road itself and they are at the other Gopalan Mall."

"Oh God, I didn't know that," I replied guiltily, biting my tongue.

After all the confusion, finally we met Bharati and Vinay at Rajarajeshwari Nagar, and went home to Vijayanagar.

While having tea and snacks, I apologized for giving incomplete information about the theatre and explained as to how and why the confusion had happened. After the meal, my husband finally asked what had puzzled us. "But Vinay, I don't understand, how were you allowed inside the theater of that mall on the ticket of this mall?"

"Uncle, in fact, the door-man didn't let us in at first. But we didn't give up. We argued vehemently and told him, 'My uncle and aunty are already inside... we have tickets, why are you stopping us?" Still, he didn't let us in, so we told, "if you want, come with us, and see for yourself..." Our raised voices were disturbing the audience sitting near the door and they started shooing us. To avoid more complaints from the audience, reluctantly - he allowed us in the theatre. The movie had already started, so instead of searching for our seats in the dark, we just sat on whichever empty seat that we found in the first row... During the interval I noticed that someone else had occupied our seats. But we decided to let it go because we didn't want to argue over seats once again..." he smiled and concluded, "so we watched the movie from the front row. Now we can say that we have seen Ranbir and Priyanka from close quarters..." Vinay told the whole story. I appreciated his sense of humour.

"Now let this be... what is done is done... I am happy that I got a chance to watch 'Barfi'... Credit goes to *Mavashi* for that..." Enjoying the dessert she said, "*Mavashi*, the food was excellent, it reminded me of my mother." Bharati graciously forgave me but I was feeling guilty.

^^^^^^^^^^^^^^^^^^^^^^^^^

The next Sunday when we went to Bharati's house for dinner, I placed a gift in her hand. On seeing this Vinay teased me "Aunty, looks as if ... you have brought a penalty for the 'Barfi' confusion..."

"You guessed it right my dear son-in-law," I said with a smile.

As soon as she opened the box, Bharati's eyes widened. "*Mavashi*, you are so sweet..."

"But will you tell me what it is?" Vinay asked impatiently.

"Oh, Wow... it's mango *barfi*, my most favourite sweet... and that too from Chitale's Sweets from Pune..."

Picking up a piece of barfi from the box, Vinay said with a beaming smile "Aunty, if the 'penalty' is so tasty and sweet, then please... create more confusion... But next time, order my favourite, Kaka Halwai's *Khova Barfi*... as penalty"

We burst out laughing and they indulged in devouring the mango barfi.

* * * * * * * * * * * * * * * * * *

* * * * * * * * * * *

VII
Prayer

Vrishali *Ajji's* (grandmother) only daughter, Sonali - also had only one daughter. Though she was named Mitali, Vrishali used to call her "Chiu"(baby sparrow in Marathi) because the sweet little girl was as chirpy and active as a baby sparrow... She was studying in the 1ˢᵗ grade and her school had Dussehra vacation, so Vrishali told Sonali, "Let Chiu stay with us for a few days during the vacation so that you would have some free time for yourself." Sonali promptly took the offer.

Chiu loved staying with her grandparents – Vrishali *Ajji* and *Ajoba* (grandfather). Of course, it was a challenge for them to keep an eye on their naughty grand-daughter. Chiu was peaceful only when she was asleep. Once she woke up, she loved to explore every nook and corner of the house - especially Ajji's curio cupboard. It was like a little treasure for her. Ajji had displayed some rare and expensive items in that. She wouldn't let Chiu touch any of the items in the cupboard. So, when Ajji was away Chiu would stand on a stool, and one by one pick up everything curiously. She would even try to rearrange them when Ajji was not around...

But when Chiu was bored with pranks, she would help Ajji in cooking. She would go for morning walks with Ajoba, and return with flowers, leaves, seeds, feathers that she had picked up while walking. She would eat her favourite foods and also Ajji's favourite foods. Ajoba would play with her and Ajji would even dance with her.

Grandmother and Granddaughter shared a great bonding. Ajji had placed some pots of flowering plants in the living room balcony. She used to call that balcony 'Lalbagh'; and the 3 feet diameter plastic tub - in which Ajoba had left some fish - as 'Lotus-pond' !!! From time to time, beautiful lotus flowers would bloom in it.

Every morning, when Ajji and Ajoba sat on the balcony and had their tea, Chiu drank milk without making any fuss. She used to shout good morning from the balcony to Ajoba's friends walking down the driveway. After the 'tea ceremony', Ajji watered the plants and Ajoba fed the fish. The fishes were so small that they could not swallow even small grains - the size of sago. They would just lick the grains which floated back and forth. When the grains became smaller the fishes would swallow it. Chiu just loved to sit there and watch till the fishes finished eating all the grains.

One morning, while sitting on the balcony watching the fish, Chiu suddenly exclaimed,

"Ajji, why is Blackie swimming horizontally?" Blackie was Chiu's favourite fish.

Ajji looked at it. She wondered how come she didn't notice that dead fish in the morning... Maybe it was covered by lotus leaf... she thought to herself. But she told Chiu,

"I think it is unwell, don't you worry Chiu, once it recovers, it will swim properly" Chiu believed the explanation and went for her morning-walk with her grandfather. Before going to buy vegetables, Ajoba dropped her at home. After sometime Ajji realized that though Chiu had come home, there was no activity or any sound. Ajji wondered what prank Chiu was up to!

She searched all the rooms in their three-bedroom apartment... under the beds, behind the doors, even inside the wardrobe, but Chiu was not to be seen. She checked the main door, but it was bolted... that means, she was somewhere in the house... but where? Ajji was getting worried now.

Suddenly she noticed that the curtains of the living room were closed.

'I remember clearly... I opened it in the morning... Who closed it again?' Saying this, she opened the curtains and saw Chiu - sitting peacefully on a stool in the balcony, facing the pond. Her eyes were closed and she was muttering something. Ajji felt so relieved that Chiu was not lost that she just returned to the kitchen without disturbing Chiu.

That day, Chiu ate her lunch quietly. Everything that was served on her plate was eaten without any fuss. Post lunch, she went to the bedroom, read a storybook, scribbled abstracts in her drawing book and fell asleep...

"What has happened to Chiu today? Why is she so silent?" Ajji asked Ajoba without expecting any answer.

^^^^^^^^^^^^^^^^^^

After getting up from her nap, Chiu went back to the balcony.

"Ajji, I can't see Blackie..."

"He must be resting Chiu... he is unwell, isn't it...?"

"Ajji, but when will he get better?" she asked in a sad voice.

" Mostly by tomorrow." Grandma said.

"Is that so, Ajoba?" she asked. Ajji signalled Ajoba with her eyes.

"Yes, yes, I feel the same way," he said. Satisfied with confirmation from Ajoba, Chiu went to play with her friends.

"I think Chiu is very disturbed because she can't see the fish..." said Ajoba.

^^^^^^^^^^^^^^^^^^^

Chiu got up early the next day and went first to the balcony, saying, "Ajoba, let us feed the fish". He replied, "But Mitali, the fish is fed only once a day... at 8 o'clock, when you drink milk, isn't it? Right now, it's only 6 o'clock..."

"But please Ajoba... poor Blackie is starving since yesterday, he hasn't eaten anything," Chiu pleaded so much that Ajoba sprinkled a spoonful of grains into the pond. As the fish came up, Chiu shouted,

"Hey Ajji, come quickly, Blackie is fine and swimming, look how happy he is..."

"Indeed, Chiu... Wow... how quickly he has recovered..." Ajji joined in Chiu's excitement.

"Yes!!! ... Do you know Ajji?... Yesterday I prayed to God and told him to cure Blackie... Remember? You had told me that when we pray, God listens and then fulfils our wishes..." chirped Chiu.

"Yes my dear... you are so smart," said Ajji, hugging Chiu.

Leaving Chiu on the balcony, Ajoba called Ajji inside the house. "I want to talk to you. What you did just now was not right, you should have told her the truth" said Ajoba, blaming Ajji.

"Yes...but I couldn't do it," Ajji said in a low voice.

^^^^^^^^^^^^^^^^^^

Dussehra vacation was soon over and Sonali came to pick up Chiu.

"I will get bored when you are gone Chiu," Ajji said.

"But Ajji, Ajoba will be here to give you company, and besides that, I'll call you every Friday after school" Chiu smiled sweetly at Ajji.

She kept her promise, but last two Fridays she didn't call, only Sonali spoke on the phone. Ajji was worried.

"Sonu, why isn't Chiu calling?" she rang up and asked Sonali.

"Oh... that... because she doesn't have time, Mummy... after returning from school, she freshens up and goes straight to the Pooja room. Then recites '*Shubham Karoti*' and some other prayers with closed eyes... Don't you worry, she is fine. I will tell her to call you" said Sonali.

"Oh, ok... but what is she praying so much for?" Vrishali was curious to know.

"Not for what... Instead ask, for whom..." said Sonali. "Her favourite teacher has been in the hospital for the past fifteen days. So Mituli is praying for her speedy recovery."

"Oh! is it Miss Arti?"

"Yes, but how do you know Arti Madam?"

"Heard a lot about her from Chiu.... What happened to her?" Vrishali's voice was concerned.

"I don't know exactly... but it seems like something serious." Sonali continued, "Chiu told me that you had told her that 'God fulfils the wishes of those who pray... so she is praying sincerely every evening."

Not knowing what to say, Vrishali just said, "Well, well... let it be," and hung up the phone.

"Why are you in such a mood? What did Sonali say?" Ajoba asked.

Vrishali told him about her conversation with Sonali.

"I had told you, to tell the truth to Mitali." He said accusingly but Vrishali did not reply. She was witnessing the turmoil of conflicting thoughts... the arguments and counterarguments... between her heart and her brain...

Her heart said,

"I didn't want to tell her the truth that Blackie was dead - for three reasons. The first reason was 'worry' - whether a six-year-old girl could withstand the fact that Blackie was dead... Second reason was - how to explain the concept of death to a six-year-old who has just begun to understand life... And the third reason was the satisfaction of being able to impress the importance of prayer... at least for Blackie's sake, Chiu started praying ... I am happy that Chiu wouldn't be an atheist like her mother... And anyway, I didn't tell her that the fish she saw was Blackie; so, I didn't lie to Chiu..." the heart presented his side vehemently.

"Wow, you - who taught Chiu- 'to always tell the truth and nothing but the truth'... are you saying this?" challenged the brain. "Agreed... that you didn't tell a lie, you didn't say that the fish she saw was Blackie; but you didn't tell the truth either... Similar to *'Naro wa Kunjrova'* said by Dharmaraja to Dronacharya in the *Kurukshetra* war... Whatever explanation you might give in defence, but I would still call it a lie..."

The heart was listening intently as the brain continued to speak.

"Remember one thing Vrishali, faith in God due to misunderstanding does not last forever... Do you understand that- if that faith is shaken up - for whatever reason - Chiu's faith in you would also be shattered? As of now, she believes that her teacher would recover - solely due to her prayers – just like Blackie recovered. But; by chance, if Miss Arti does not recover, Chiu's faith in prayer and in you, both would be shattered... and – *God forbid* - it can happen anytime..."

"Oh... No... no ... "Vrishali began to plead earnestly.

"What's up Ajji, what's going on?" Ajoba asked teasingly.

"Me?... no... what...? nothing," she blabbered and turned towards the kitchen. Her mind was very disturbed with the thought, 'Would Arti madam recover? Sonu said she was serious...'

^^^^^^^^^^^^^^^^^^^^^^^^^

Just before the Christmas vacation, Sonali called.

"Mummy, we are going to Trivandrum for a week during this vacation."

"That's good. The weather there should be good now." Vrishali said. After talking about other things, she asked the question that had been bothering her.

"I wanted to ask you Sonu... how is that Aarti madam?"

"She is better, she will come to school from January."
'Oh, Thank god..."
Sonali couldn't understand why her mother was so relieved...

^^^^^^^^^^^^^^^^^^^^^

Vrishali didn't call Sonali during February and March because those were busy months. Sonali was super-busy with bank's year-end work and Chiu with studies for the annual exam. In April, when the school results were announced, Vrishali called to enquire if Chiu's result had come. Sonali said, "Results are here. She has got sixth rank."

"How come sixth rank in the annual exam? She got second rank in the half-term exam, isn't it Sonu? What happened?"

"Hmm... Actually, I expected it, Mummy... Because Chiu hardly studied for the final exam... she was just 'praying' to get the first rank. She thinks that prayer can do wonders... she is convinced that it was because of her prayers that Arti madam got better... I tried to explain, but she didn't listen. Finally, I gave up... Since it was just the first-grade exam, I didn't nag her too much." Sonali said.

Vrishali could sense the sadness in Sonali's voice. "How about sending Chiu to our home during the summer vacation?" she asked.

"Sure, I will send her. Because of that result, she was upset for a few days. But slowly she will be back on the track... We will come next Saturday."

^^^^^^^^^^^^^^^^

On Saturday afternoon, Sonali, Mitali and Shantanu enjoyed the delicious lunch that Vrishali had prepared. In the evening all of them had dinner at a restaurant and then Sonali and Shantanu returned home, leaving Mithali with her grandparents.

The next morning as usual, Chiu sat in the balcony. She had her milk while Ajji-Ajoba enjoyed hot tea and the fish had their food. Ajoba enquired about Chiu's friends, her favorite cartoons etc.

And then, pretending to know nothing, Vrishali asked Chiu, "Hey Chiu, I forgot to ask, did you get your exam result? What rank did you get?"

"What is there to ask? First rank..., right Mitali?" said Ajoba.

"... No Ajoba, I got sixth rank." Chiu replied in a small voice, without looking at them.

"... But Ajji, how could this happen? I had prayed every day to get the first rank," said Chiu in a hurt voice.

"Well, you prayed, but... did you study?" Ajji asked in a soft voice.

Chiu just kept mum.

Then Ajji continued, "Look Chiu, just praying will not do. First, you must study. God helps only those, who work hard, and then pray... means, first you do your best, and then leave the rest to God... ok?"

Chiu listened attentively. She was shaking her head as some thoughts crossed her mind... Finally, she asked,

"But then, how come our teacher was healed just by prayer, Ajji? All the boys and girls in my class and I too, prayed to God for her to get cured..."

"Yes, your prayers also helped, but let's not forget the doctors who treated her, the teacher's family that took good care of her... That was as important as prayer... As a result of their efforts and your prayers - that she got better. Not just by your prayer..." Ajji explained her point.

"Hmm..." Chiu nodded in agreement, yet she had a doubt in her mind.

"But Ajji, you remember, once a fish in your lotus pond - my favourite Blackie – had fallen ill. At that time, no medicine was given to him. I just prayed ... and the next day he recovered and began to swim so well."

There was pride in Chiu's voice as she said this.

Ajoba signaled Ajji. She got the hint - this is the moment she should grab to tell the truth.

"Chiu, I think, the time has come to tell you the truth... Yes, I remember what happened to Blackie." Choosing her words carefully, she said, "I must confess that, I lied to you that day... because I thought you'd be upset if I told you the truth...In reality, that day the fish was not sick, it was dead..." After sharing the facts with Chiu, she felt as free as a kite flying without a thread. She eagerly waited for Chiu's reaction.

After a few moments of silence, Chiu asked seriously, "Dead means... similar to - when my friend's dog Tommy died and was never seen again... is that right Ajji?"

"Yes... yes," replied Ajji.

"But... the next day I saw the fish... How was that possible?" Chiu was confused and curious to know.

"It was a similar looking new fish bought by Ajoba." Ajji blurted out solving the mystery.

"Similar to when my Barbie doll broke and you got me a new one, Ajoba bought a new fish... Is that right Ajji?" Chiu asked.

"Yeah, right," said Ajji.

Without saying anything, Chiu once again sat in silence. Her little brain was working hard.

"That means, prayer is of no use Ajji?" Chiu asked at last, in a hurt voice.

"No, it's not like that Chiu. I'll explain it this way... Let me give you an example. Tomorrow we have plans to visit Mysore, you know that, right? Suppose, after sitting in the car, Ajoba just prays 'Dear God, please take us safely to Mysore.' Do you think that by just saying that prayer, we would automatically reach safely to Mysore?"

Just the thought of a car - driving itself - like the flying carpet of Aladdin, made Chiu laugh.

"Would we reach Mysore automatically by just praying?" Ajji repeated her question, then said, "You know the answer, isn't it? we can't reach Mysore automatically – just by praying. For that, Ajoba has to drive the car and follow the road safety rules; only then we would reach Mysore safely... yes, or no?"

"Yes," Chiu nodded.

"So, just like that, to achieve any success you should not rely only on prayer; but you have to work hard also."

"Ok Ajji, I understood." She clapped her hands. "First study and then pray. Right?"

"Exactly," said Ajji.

Satisfied with her efforts to convince Chiu about prayer, she got up smilingly.

Her face was glowing with happiness because she had succeeded in dispelling Chiu's misunderstanding about prayer without losing her faith in prayer.

The conflict between Vrishali's brain and heart was over at last.

* * * * * * * * * * * * * * * * * * *

* * * * * * * * * * * * * * *

VIII
Virus

Bhanudev Maharaj's morning sermon was over. People came to him in a queue, bowed and moved away. He blessed each and every devotee by placing his hand on their head. Shambhu was standing in the same queue. As he approached Maharaj, he prostrated.

"Oh, get up son, this type of salutation is only for God." He helped him to get up and blessed him, but Shambhu just stood there, without moving forward.

"Is there something you want to talk about?" Bhanudev Maharaj asked.

Shambhu just nodded.

"Then come back later."

So, Shambhu went to meet him after Maharaj's rest time was over. He bowed down and stood silently.

Maharaj recognized him and asked, "I think ... you wanted to speak to me. What is it about?"

"Maharaj, I am Shambhu, I want to stay in your Ashram and be a *sadhak* (devotee)" He said in one breath.

For a moment, Maharaj was surprised by Shambhu's straightforward reply. Perhaps he was the first person to tell his intention in so few words.

"Why?" he asked.

"Because my heart is weary of the world. I want to be a seeker."

"- Seeker? Hm... It's not that easy, but let me think..." "Suppose you stay here, how can you make yourself useful to the Ashram?" Maharaj asked him.

"Maharaj, I am a carpenter... I can help in the construction work of the Ashram and I am willing to do any other work that Maharaj wishes me to do... but let me stay here" pleaded Shambhu.

"Does your family approve of your decision? And what about your present job?"

" I have left my job and I am single."

Maharaj just listened without any comment, so Shambhu continued. "Sir, in the past few years, I have not only read your books, but I have participated in workshops also. It gave a lot of relief to my disturbed mind, so I came to your Ashram. And after listening to your sermons... I decided to become a seeker. "

"I told you just now that it's not that simple." Maharaj told the conditions of living in the Ashram.

"Shambhu, let me be very clear. For living here, you have to fulfil certain conditions. First condition is, even if you work here, you will not get any remuneration. You have to work as a volunteer, whatever the job may be. In return, the Ashram will take care of your accommodation and food. Second condition is... the discipline of the Ashram must be followed without any questions. And most important... the third condition. I will decide when to initiate you as a seeker and that may take years... because it will depend on your overall conduct... Are you agreeable to all this?"

"Yes Maharaj, I accept all the conditions. I assure you that I would not give any chance for complaints," promised Shambhu, folding his hands once again.

Bhanudev nodded and on the same day, recruited him as a volunteer in the Ashram.

Considering Shambhu's carpentry experience, Sukhdev, the manager of the Ashram, assigned him the task of supervising workers who made doors, windows, furniture etc. for the additional residential accommodation under construction. Apart from that, Sukhdev would assign him odd jobs like helping in the kitchen or maintaining the cleanliness of the Ashram etc. In this busy schedule of every day, Shambhu could steal some free time in which he would listen to sermons or read books. Within three years, the soft-spoken but highly committed Shambhu became Sukhdev's right-hand man.

Although Bhanudev Maharaj toured all over India for eight months of the year to deliver sermons, four months of *Chaturmas*, he spent in the Ashram. Visiting the Ashram during that period gave double benefit to his devotees - seeing Maharaj in person and listening to his discourses. To take advantage of this, many people thronged the Ashram during those four months. At that time, all the senior volunteers were on the job of maintaining law and order in the Ashram.

After a three-year internship, in the fourth year - Shambhu was tasked with controlling the crowd in the "Discourse Hall".

∧∧∧∧∧∧∧∧∧∧∧∧∧∧∧∧∧∧∧∧∧∧

That day- like every other day of *Chaturmas*, the hall was brimming with people. As Bhanudev Maharaj entered the hall, all the whispering sound stopped. He occupied his ornate chair on the dais. Shambhu, who was standing in the aisle, signalled to the crowd - who stood respectfully to welcome Maharaj - to sit down.

And just then, he saw 'her'. He looked carefully again.

'Could it be Kamli?... But ... how could it be?' ... His mind wandered away from the sermon. Just like sediment at the bottom would rise to the surface when a stone is thrown in the pond, old memories surfaced in Shambhu's mind.

^^^^^^^^^^^^^^^^^^^^^^^^^^^^^

He was married to Kamli ten years ago. He remembered how they had met...

In an accident at a construction site, Shambhu was injured when the scaffolding – erected for the slab – collapsed. Since his backbone was affected badly, he had to remain under hospital care - at least for a month. Kamli was a nurse at the hospital where he was taken. Her duty was in Shambhu's ward. Just for time-pass, he started observing other patients, doctors, nurses and everything else. He admired Kamli for her sincerity and commitment. She followed the doctor's instructions to the last "T". Generally, she talked to the patients kindly, but she also knew how to handle the non-cooperative patients... She was smart and youthful.

He liked her and had a gut-feeling that she knew it!

So, on the day of discharge, he told Kamli in front of others,

"Sister, I like you... but not as a "sister..." He paused and smiled.

"Would you like to be my wife and spend the rest of your life with me?"

Kamali didn't know how to react to that unexpected question... The other patients' eyes were fixed on her. She didn't answer but she blushed... And he got his answer.

One day after a few months of their marriage, he suggested that she need not work as a nurse because he was earning well. She refused. He was upset. She tried to convince him. "Having additional income is always useful in times of trouble." She said.

But he was not convinced. Thinking that 'the money he earned is not enough for Kamli', he got a job in a Gulf country without her knowledge.

"I didn't mean that your income is not enough, please don't go, we got married only one year back..." she begged him, but he went to the Gulf despite Kamali's plea.

"To do the same work that I do here, I would get paid many times more there. I will send the money, then you leave this job. Besides, the agent has told, that you can join after a year, don't you worry," he had convinced Kamli.

But the reality was very different. After deducting food and lodging expenses from the salary, there was hardly any money left. Four years had passed since he left India and was away from Kamli. The only communication between them was through occasional phone calls, but that was not enough. She continued with her job, because he could not answer her question...'You are not here, what can I do all day sitting at home?'

Disillusioned about the glamour of the Gulf, he got tired of his job in a few years. He decided to quit and return to India. But the employer was not willing to return his passport. Travel was impossible without a passport. He came to know that like him, there were other workers who were misled and trapped by the agent's false promises. One of the supervisors managed to get Shambhu's passport back, but Shambhu had to pay a heavy price. Some of the saved money was spent on the ticket and the rest had to be paid to the supervisor who procured the passport.

He returned to his hometown in India in a disheartened state. Five years were wasted running after a mirage... and he had returned home penniless.

He went home, but the house was locked; so, he went to the hospital to meet Kamli. He didn't find her in the ward so he peeped into the nurses' room, and was shocked...

- He couldn't believe his eyes...What was he looking at?

Sadness, humiliation, contempt, deception... so many depressing emotions crowded in Shambhu's mind.

"What have I achieved in five years? – Nothing but misery -Instead of gaining something, I have lost a lot for the sake of that job... Precious five years of family life... my sanity... my earnings... and now my wife...? I am a loser..." He was terribly angry... with himself, with Kamli, with the entire world.

He headed to the station without speaking a word to Kamali, boarded the train which was about to leave and deboarded at the last station.

No one knew him in that city. Unknown city, unknown people - but he couldn't escape from the same old sorrow, the same old pain –

^ ^ ^ ^ ^ ^ ^ ^ ^ ^ ^ ^ ^ ^

"What's that sound?" Shambhu looked around with a jerk. He realized that people were chanting the Aarti. Once again, his eyes drifted to 'her'. She too was staring at him. He was convinced that 'she' was Kamli. Avoiding her gaze, he stood at the door, managing the crowd.

After everyone left, she came to the door and asked him, "Are you Mr. Shambhu Thorat from Pune?"

"No," he said curtly and went outside the hall. Standing far away in the courtyard, he could see Kamli talking to Sukhdev.

"Go to hell... let her talk to anyone she wants. I'm done with her." Shambhu muttered to himself.

He was relieved when he did not see Kamli at the next morning's sermon. "I think she must have left... Pain in the neck...Good riddance..." he said to himself.

During lunchtime, Sukhdev informed Shambhu that Maharaj wants to meet him in the afternoon. So, he went to Bhanudev's cottage.

Maharaj's face was more serious than usual. He didn't waste time beating around the bush and came straight to the point – just like Shambhu...

"Shambhu, I remember, when you came here you told me that you were single. But yesterday a woman named Kamli met Sukhdev and told him that you are her missing husband..."

Shambhu stood with his head down without showing any reaction.

"Shambhu, I want to know the truth... Why did you tell a lie? You have broken the basic rule of the Ashram. Remember, every lie gets exposed sooner or later, so better to tell the truth - at least now. Who is that woman? Why does she say that you were married to her?" He could feel the anger in Bhanudev's voice.

Shambhu felt ashamed. Slowly, his face turned angry. Bhanudev was observing him.

Controlling his disgust about Kamli, he apologized for hiding the truth and narrated his life story – meeting Kamli - marriage - job in the Gulf - returning bankrupt - and the incident in the hospital...

Maharaj listened patiently and said, "Why didn't you talk to her that day, in the hospital? You left with fury in your head. That was a grave mistake. Go, talk to her now – Correct the mistakes of your past life."

Shambhu had no option but to obey Maharaj's order. With permission from Sukhdev, he skipped attending the evening sermon of that day. Instead, he went to Kamli's room to meet her. She opened the door. As soon as he entered, he began to bombard, "Why did you come here? Are you not ashamed? And where is that old doctor? He hasn't come, has he?" She listened to his outburst quietly.

He continued disdainfully, "On that day, I had returned to India... I was so eager to meet you, to hug you after so many years of separation - but the house was locked so I went to the hospital... And I saw what I could never imagine... you were crying, and instead of me, that doctor was caressing you - on your shoulders... What was happening there?"

His voice had become shrill. "Why did you come here? Why did you complain about me to Maharaj? Let me live here peacefully. Go back. Got it? Go back and never come again, I don't ever want to see your face... " He opened the door to leave.

" Okay, you may go." Kamli said calmly. " I will tell your Maharaj that you are still unwilling to listen to my explanation."

Angrily, Shambhu stopped at the door. She didn't say anything.

"Then explain what you want to..." he growled.

She started with a sigh. "It was barely a year after our wedding... How much I begged you not to leave - but you left me for the lure of money... You have no idea how I managed to live alone during those five years - You didn't care about it, but my senior doctor did. He was like an elder brother to me. He used to console me whenever I was depressed. He knew that I was working mechanically... I missed you so much..." She was experiencing that pain again.

"That day when you saw us, the doctor was assuring me that he would get me a job as a nurse in the same country where you had gone. And because he put the word out, I got a job there. Within a couple of months, I went to that unknown country. More than the excitement of the new job, it was the joy of meeting you...I thought, even if our workplaces were in different cities, we can be together at least on holidays, my dream of a family will be fulfilled..."

Listening to her, Shambhu's anger was melting.

"... But it was not meant to be... When I looked for you, I found out that you had already returned to India. I was terribly disappointed... Though I wanted to, I could not return immediately, because I had to complete my three-year contract.There was heavy fine for breaking the contract. So, I had to remain there – I called you so many times, but you never answered even once."

Her eyes were moist. He listened silently. He could feel the pain, sorrow, despair in her voice... and he was responsible for that. He felt guilty.

"I came here with my friend for some peace of mind, and happened to see you. Even if you have grown a beard and moustache, I recognized you, but you denied – Do you realize Shambhu, that in fact you had denied your own identity – when you said you weren't Shambhu Thorat... But I was sure, so I told the manager about you and he told Maharaj" – She was sobbing. "I didn't want to lose you again – so I talked to him... Did I make a mistake?"

Shambhu was speechless. The thick fog of misunderstanding had dissipated.

He hugged her, "No dear Kamli... It was my mistake...please forgive me" he pleaded sincerely.

He wondered how to tell Maharaj that he had patched up with Kamli, that he wanted to leave the Ashram and live with his wife...

The next morning both of them went to meet Bhanudev Maharaj. After bowing to him, Shambhu just stood there. He did not know what to say, how to say...

But Maharaj welcomed them wholeheartedly. Smiling lovingly, he said, "Shambhu, I wanted to initiate you as a Sadhak this year. But it looks like your plan to become a Sadhak has been cancelled... Let it be. The right time has to come for that... it hasn't come yet." Seeing his affectionate gaze, Shambhu smiled shyly. He was amazed how Maharaj had read his mind. With great reverence, both of them bowed down to him.

He blessed them, paused for a while and said seriously, "Remember one thing Shambhu. A harmful *Kida* (bug) can multiply and destroy a whole jungle - if not killed instantly. Similarly, the 'virus of doubt' can multiply and finish any relationship... so, it must be exterminated at once. If you had debugged your mind in time, both of you need not have suffered so much. Now go home and start a new life. Be happy... and yes... Keep away from every virus"...

Shambhu pledged by placing his hand on Kamli's head, and said, "Ji Maharaj..."

* * * * * * * * * * * * * * * * * *

* * * * * * * * * * * *

IX
Confession

Although they argued very often, the topics varied.

That day's topic of argument was "Their 25th wedding anniversary". She just wanted to offer a pooja in the temple and keep it a low-key celebration. But he wanted to invite everybody and make it a gala function... Tired of listening to this argument for an hour, their only son suggested, "Why don't you do this? Go to the temple and perform pooja-abhishekam in the morning and throw a party in the evening for the near and dear ones."

Both of them, tired of arguing, readily agreed to this suggestion.

His clients, her colleagues, members from his club, her kitty friends, their son's circle of friends, and their relatives and neighbours... the list of invitees became longer and longer, like Lord Maruti's tail. Finally, they had to book a large hall for that – a so-called simple function– which was supposed to be for the closest people.

However, at the end of the day both were happy because the function went off well and every one whom they had invited, graced the occasion.

When they came home, their son placed an envelope in their hands. "A little gift from me - for your 25th wedding anniversary."

"Oh, what's the need to give a gift? To have an understanding, loving son like you is the greatest gift to us..." She said sweetly.

"Then please accept this gift from your loving son" He smiled and said, "I have booked you both for Bhutan tour! Enjoy and have a good time. I love you Ma, love you Dad," he said.

^^^^^^^^^^^^^^^^^^^^^^^^^^^^

Both were exhausted after the long journey - from Bangalore to Bhutan. As soon as they checked in the hotel, she changed into night clothes and lay down on the bed, but he continued to sit on the chair, staring at the ceiling, engrossed in his own thoughts...

"Hey, Mr. Sadanand Gore, we are on vacation, what are you thinking about so deeply?" she asked.

"I want to tell you something." He said with a serious face.

"It is quite late, let us relax... you can tell me tomorrow"

"No," he said firmly. " For the last 25 years it's been bothering me, I must tell you now... Once I confess, the burden on my mind will go."

"Confession? ...About what?" She asked, trying to keep her eyes open.

"You don't know, but before we got married, I was in love... for three months and thirteen days." He blurted out the headline.

It had the right effect. She sat up; eyes wide open.

"Three months and thirteen days... you mean... you remember so much in detail about that love?"

"Yes, I remember it well, because, after three months and thirteen days, I got married..." he said with a sigh.

Her sleepiness vanished instantly.

"What happened was," he started narrating. "Those days, I was working in Calcutta. Mom, dad, grandma, everybody was telling me – 'We worry about you all the time because you stay alone - so far away - eat outside food every day – it's not healthy - so, get married – your wife will be there to look after you and our worries will be over' etc. - Whenever this topic came up, I used a different excuse each time to avoid getting married. Once, I got an extended weekend holiday, so I came to Bangalore. My mother was just waiting to get my approval for a *'proposal'*. She said they had seen the girl and had liked her and since I was in Bangalore, I should meet her too..."

" I told her point blank, 'I don't like this custom of 'seeing' girls. Why should girls be treated like objects? Is it right to go to her house, have tea and snacks free of cost and then reject the girl brazenly... wouldn't she feel hurt? How would 'you' feel if someone rejects your son like that?" Mom and dad could not argue with me and did not discuss any further about that proposal. Though I sounded rude, I did not want to hurt them, so later, I talked to them casually and gathered some information about that girl - like where she worked, what her qualification was etc."

"Then I spoke to Ravi Gokhale, - my friend - yes, you know him too. The next morning, as prearranged, Ravi and I set out to 'see' the girl. I went to the bank where she worked and Ravi went to the shop in front of the bank. I sat, occupying a strategic position, overlooking the manager's cabin. At exactly 10 o'clock, as per our plan, the cabin phone rang. The Manager called the peon, told him something and kept the receiver aside. Then a young girl came to pick up the phone and... I'll tell you what ..."

"As soon as I saw her, my heart stopped for a moment... then it started beating faster! I had fallen in love with her... Love at first sight... When I came home, I solemnly apologized for being rude, and announced that I had thought it over and was ready to marry the girl they had proposed to."

"But without seeing the girl?" dad asked, to which I replied, "You have liked her, and approved her, that's enough for me. Go ahead."

The very next day I returned to Calcutta.

^ ^ ^ ^ ^ ^ ^ ^ ^ ^ ^ ^ ^

The wedding day was after 3 months and 13 days.

He stopped for a few moments lost in thoughts, and then continued "During *Seemant Pujan*, Guruji called the bride on the stage and I was shocked...she was not my dream girl... the bride was someone else."

"...You mean me...?" She asked in disbelief.

"Yes" he said, avoiding her gaze.

"Do you still miss her?" She asked in a hurt tone.

"Sometimes... sometimes I do," he admitted honestly.

"But then how come you didn't recognize her? She had come to our 25th Wedding Anniversary. I was the one who invited her... on purpose."

"You mean... you knew about her all along?"

"Yes" she said with a mischievous smile.

"Now let me tell you my side of the story... It so happened, there was a discussion about your 'proposal' in our house too. My mother had asked me to take leave and stay back at home that day. She said that you had come to Bangalore and may return the next day... so, you might come to 'see' me. But you didn't come... Instead, a message came in the evening from your family... to start preparations for the wedding."

"Everyone was happy... but I felt that something was not right and that 'something' was bothering me."

"The next day, when I went to the bank, the manager said, "Madam, there was a call for you yesterday about one customer's savings account. Savita Joshi attended. Get the details from her.""

"Savita talked about the phone and said, "Sunanda, I must tell you something strange that happened yesterday. A man had come and he was sitting right here - in front of the counter. When I asked, does he have any query, he said, he was waiting for a friend. Then the Manager called me to attend the call, but I noticed from his cabin that the man simply got up after some time and left... no friend came... I think he came just to enjoy AC ... What sort of people..." I didn't listen to her further comments... because suddenly everything had fallen in place... Do you know what happened?"

He looked confused... so she explained.

"That day your friend Ravi called Sunanda Vartak on the phone to inquire about his account, but I was on leave. So, my boss must have called Savita... AND ..." She said with a faint smile, "You mistook the beautiful, slim, glorious Savita Joshi... for me... Sunanda Vartak.".

Then, pausing for a moment, she said solemnly "Today, I also have a confession to make. I had realised the mix-up... I really wanted to clear your misunderstanding... but I didn't... I kept mum... Because I had fallen in love with you... just by seeing your photo...that your mother had given when they had come to our house..." She blushed. "So, ... to compensate for your 'loss', I invited her on our 25th wedding anniversary. After all, I got you as my husband because of her... Isn't it?"

"But did she really come? Then you should have at least introduced me to her." He said complainingly.

"Oh darling... I forgot. But I have taken a photo with her, I'll show you. Here, see this... This is her and this is her husband... third husband." Sunanda showed a mobile photo taken with a fat woman.

"... I can't believe... Is this really her?... And her 'third' husband?" he stared at the photo for a long time. His face changed expressions which she could read easily... After all they were married for 25 years. He finally had a hearty laugh.

"Let it go now... It's late, let's sleep. And yes, after we go back, don't forget to thank that Savita, on my behalf too..."

She looked at him questioningly.

Hugging her lovingly, he said, "Though indirectly, she was instrumental in our marriage. That's why I too want to thank her. After all, ... I got you as my wife because of her... didn't I?"

* * * * * * * * * * * * * * * * * *

* * * * * * * * * * * *

X

Destiny

Morning hours are generally rush hours as I am busy cooking breakfast, lunch etc. in the kitchen. So, when my mobile phone rang that morning, I just glanced at the number. It was from some unknown caller, so I ignored it. But when it rang for the third time, I picked it up wondering who it could be?

"Hello, am I speaking to Katkar madam?" the caller asked.

"Yes, speaking..."

"Madam, I'm Vanita – speaking from Kammanahalli. I am Suli's neighbour. Suli has gone..."

"Ah, where did she go?" I asked.

"To God's abode... I thought that I must inform you, so I called..."

I couldn't believe what I had heard.

"What are you talking about...?" I asked after recovering from the initial shock, but the phone was cut by then.

"Whose call was that? Why are you standing like a pillar?" - looking up from the newspaper, my husband asked in an irritated voice, "The cooker is whistling, should the gas be reduced or turned off?"

"Turn off the gas... And can you book an Ola cab for me?I want to go to Kammanahalli. Sulu passed away..."

As the taxi picked up speed, I got lost in the memory of Sulu...

^^^^^^^^^^^^^^^^^^^^

The first time I saw her was at the Chowdiah Memorial Hall.

I was a teacher in a Government School. The State Government used to organise a cultural get together –'Sneh-Sammelan' – every year during Diwali holidays. The participants were the teachers of all the government schools in the state. That year there was a 'One-Act-drama' competition. Sulu's school staged a drama based on 'adult education' in a village. The drama as such was nothing great, but the main character- "Chinni" - was very refreshing. The happy-go-lucky twentyish 'Chinni' who wanders around the village merrily, attends school occasionally, mocks the teachers, and eventually falls in love with a teacher... shy yet bubbly Chinni, won the hearts of the audience. Of course, the best actress award was won by Sulochana Gowda who portrayed 'Chinni'.

"What brilliant acting by your Sulochana madam..." I told the headmistress of her school. "Yes–" she said nonchalantly and started talking to someone else.

∧∧∧∧∧∧∧∧∧∧∧∧∧∧∧∧∧∧∧∧∧∧

After the holidays, once again I got caught up in the routine of completing syllabus portions, exams, papers, results, vacation... Slowly the memory of Sneh-Sammelan and Chinni faded.

But, it revived when I saw her, as a Manipuri dancer in the Group Dance competition at the next year's annual get-together. Her gentle smile and graceful steps earned her the best dancer award. I was totally amazed by her multiple skills... She could portray both characters – of a belligerent village girl Chinni and the graceful, dainty Manipuri dancer... a world of difference between them... played equally well and convincingly...

I was so charmed and impressed by her that after the crowd of admirers around her subsided, I went to meet her. I congratulated her and introduced myself.

When I came away, her headmistress approached me carrying a plate of food in her hand. After chit chatting for a while, she advised me, "I saw you talking to that Gowda Madam. Don't fall for her charm..." And without giving any further explanation, she just got busy with the food on her plate and moved away from me.

That remark confused me, but I decided to ignore it.

∧∧∧∧∧∧∧∧∧∧∧∧∧∧∧∧∧∧

The third time I happened to see her was in Jayanagar market.

"Madam, do you recognize me? I am Sulochana Gowda." She drew my attention and said with a bright smile.

"Yes... I recognise you." I was so pleased to meet her. "Have you also come for 'Diwali' shopping?" I asked.

"Yes ma'am. Although you are from Maharashtra, you speak *Kannada* so well." She said admiring my broken *Kannada*. We exchanged some pleasantries and left. But then onwards, she started calling me once in a while. We had an age gap of twenty years, - maybe that's why she started calling me *Akka* (elder sister) and she insisted that I call her just Sulu-not Gowda Madam. In our phone conversation we spoke mostly about her school, students and parents. But sometimes she would ask doubts, and sometimes for advice. All topics were related to work and not about her family or personal life.

∧∧∧∧∧∧∧∧∧∧∧∧∧∧∧∧∧∧∧∧∧∧∧

"Madam, we have reached Kammanahalli, where to go now?" The driver brought me back to reality. Since it was a small village, we easily found Gowda Madam's house. When I reached there, the door was open and it appeared as if there was no one in the house. With hesitation, I peeped inside. A servant came to the door and said everyone has gone to the cremation ground. As I was about to board the taxi, a lady came near the taxi.

"Are you Katkar Madam?"

"Yes," I said.

"I thought so... I'm Vanita, I was the one who called you. Suli always talked about you. She had a lot of respect for you. Come in and have some tea" She said walking towards the neighbouring house. "You have travelled all the way from Bangalore... take some rest..." she said.

Though I was not in a mood for pleasantries, seeing her courteous nature, I went to her house. After offering a glass of water, she said, "it's not tea time, please have lunch and go, you have another long journey back home." and handed me a plate with *ragi-roti* (a local dish) and coconut chutney.

"It would have been a little better if I could have seen Sulu one last time," I said.

"It's good... you didn't see her," she said with a sigh, "Suli was so fair complexioned - but in the end - she had turned black-blue... That's why everything was done in such a hurry," she exclaimed.

I stopped eating halfway... food remained in my hand. But Vanita did not notice... She kept talking... like the gushing water from a dam with open gates. For the first time, I heard about Sulu's family background...

"She hailed from an educated but poor family from Mysore.When she was in her late teens, Kallappa - the son of a rich farmer, approached her father asking for Suli's hand. The fair, curly-haired Sulu liked the macho and rugged Kallappa. Soon they got married. At the time of marriage Suli had ignored that his education was only up to 9th grade. But after marriage, Suli was after him to study further. "At least pass the SSLC exam…" she begged. But Kallappa didn't believe in the importance of education. He became active in village politics and even got elected as President of a farmer's organization.

"Look, I became the president with just '9th grade pass' qualification… I will soon become a Sarpanch also. What's the use of your 'B.A., B.Ed.,' degree? You are and will always be –just a housewife…" he nagged. Suli felt offended and decided that she would teach him a lesson.

Once decided, she went all out to achieve what she wanted. After some effort, she got a job in the local Government school. She became the favourite teacher of all the students. In fact, she was my son's class-teacher when he was in the 10th grade. Besides teaching in school, she also helped parents - to apply for loans, or to fill forms… a very gentle and kind soul." she said.

"And very committed to her job… When we spoke last month, she had told me that she had become School Principal. She had a dream… to get the 'Ideal School' award. But all that is just idle talk now…" I said with a sigh.

"Yes, that's what she aimed for…. *Adarsh - Adarsh* (Ideal)" Vanita sounded a bit agitated. "That ambition of being 'Adarsh' in everything – turned out to be the cause of her death…"

"How could it be?" I was puzzled.

"Did you know that a few years back, she was honoured as best teacher? There were more senior teachers than her who had failed to get that award – They were jealous of her. Seeing her popularity with students and the parents, her husband felt inferior, because she had overtaken him… After becoming Headmistress, she became even more popular in the village than he was, so he started doubting her character, saying how she was made the Headmistress leaving behind other senior teachers. My god... their quarrels could be heard in our house. and now this... her body looked black and blue... " Vanita continued to talk looking into the blank space. Was she hinting at some foul play?

"But why would someone do such a crazy thing?" I expressed my doubt.

"Who knows?" Looking at the man outside the window, Vanita abruptly ended the subject.

I thanked her and boarded the taxi.

^^^^^^^^^^^^^^^^^^^^^^^^^

On the third day, news-paper's front page headline was, "Kammanahalli Government School Headmistress dies in suspicious circumstances. Suspect Arrested."

Although the name was not printed, I understood. After that there was no news for several months. When I called Vanita, she said that the suspect got away with the power of money and strong coercion.

Years passed by. With a heavy heart I deleted Sulu's number from my mobile. Anyway, who would call me from that number now?

^^^^^^^^^^^^^^^^^^^^^^^^^

Eventually, I retired. We left Bangalore and settled in a different city. Our new life began.

After ten years, on that day, I got a call from an unknown number again. Hesitantly, I answered the call.

"Hello Katkar madam, I'm Vanita, remember...? Your Sulu's neighbour." Immediately I recognized it.

"Oh... Yes... I remember... The taste of that roti-chutney is still on my tongue. How are you? And how's everyone at home?" I enquired casually.

"Everyone is fine."

"Your son must have finished education... What does he do now?" I asked.

"That's what I wanted to tell you. My son has become a lawyer... and he is working with a big law firm. He has got our Suli's case reopened."

I couldn't believe my ears. "Really?" I asked.

"Yes, indeed. He has vowed to bring justice to his beloved teacher... Please pray madam, – for justice – for our Suli - and for my son. That he may succeed in this endeavour."

I was so overwhelmed with feelings...

∧∧∧∧∧∧∧∧∧∧∧∧∧∧∧∧∧∧∧∧

After that, Sulu's case went on and on in court. From the two column-front page coverage of the court case, the news shrank to a small paragraph printed somewhere on the inside page and then disappeared from the newspaper.

All of a sudden - after two years - it appeared again on the front page. That day's headline read "Late justice to (late) Headmistress." The suspect was found guilty and was sentenced to life imprisonment.

Vanita's son had succeeded in getting the suspect punished. Though delayed, Suli got justice. But this was not 'the end' of Suli's story.

The breaking news in the evening telecast was -

A police jeep carrying a lifer to the main jail skidded off a bridge. The driver and the guard were injured but were saved. However, the prisoner died after hitting his head on a rock in the river and was swept away in the river... his body was never found.

That prisoner was... Kallappa.

I was stunned by that news. I couldn't help but to think...

Did *Niyati* (destiny) think that the punishment given by the 'Court of Humans' was not enough? – that he deserved a harsher punishment?

Who knows...?

* * * * * * * * * * * * * * * * *

* * * * * * * * * * * * *

XI

Too Late

Kedar Manohar Dongre, popularly known as 'K. D.' entered the "S. L. V. Production" office on the 15th floor. His tiredness and exhaustion after the rickshaw ride in the scorching heat of Hyderabad, vanished as soon as he stepped into the air-conditioned reception lobby.

The receptionist asked him to sit down, and ordered coffee for him after reading his visiting card. Sitting at the edge of the plush sofa, he began to observe the reception lobby. On one wall there were posters of all the films made by S. L. V. Production. Another wall was decorated with a mural of Tirumala Hills - with an array of awards that their films had won displayed in front of it, and the third wall was entirely a glass window...

"Sir, coffee..." said the peon who held a tray with coffee and biscuits in front of him.

Sipping hot filter coffee, Kedar's mind wandered as he gazed at the clear blue sky outside the window.

"...Once upon a time, I had dreamt of touching the sky with my name and fame... with my successful career..." he sighed. "But... success has eluded me... my feet are still shaky... my career is still unstable... how can I take-off to reach this sky?... would it remain a faraway dream?" he thought nervously.

^^^^^^^^^^^^^^^^^^^^^^^^^

He remembered... After completing his degree course in Sound Engineering, Kedar had worked in an advertising company for two and a half years. He had composed music for a few commercials during his internship. But being a trainee there, he was not given any credit for those ads. It went to his team leader and the company. However, 'Lady Luck' smiled on him when all his seniors were preoccupied with some work or the other. On that day, Kedar got an opportunity to give a presentation of a Lipstick advertisement. Mr. Malhotra, who was the Company's esteemed client, had come to see the product advertisement. He liked Kedar's proposal and presentation style also. He noticed how well Kedar had integrated music and visuals in the ad. He was impressed with Kedar's sincerity and the hard work that had gone into making an attractive ad for his product. So next time, for his company's shampoo-advertisement, he approached Kedar directly. That was his first independent assignment. He prayed to God and left for the recording studio with his parents' blessings.

With a lot of hope and giving his best to the project, Kedar recorded his first jingle. Mr. Malhotra approved it, the market received it well and the sale of the company's shampoo increased. After that success, Kedar started getting regular advertising work for all other products of Mr. Malhotra's company.

Once, at the launch event for a new product, Mr. Malhotra invited Kedar too. At that party, Mr. Malhotra introduced him to other guests and also to his daughter, Reena. Her ambition was to expand her father's company and Kedar's ambition was to become a great musician. Of course, it didn't take long for their tunes to match. Once Reena told him, "Kedar, Papa has a friend called Sharmaji, and he wants to meet you..."

"Sharma ji...he had come to your new product launch party, right?"

"Yes, that's right. But how come you remember him? It's been a long time since the party... " Reena said.

In response, Kedar just smiled and said, "Yes, I will meet him, any special reason?"

He didn't want to tell her that remembering 'probable' clients was important for expanding business...

"He wants to produce a film; I think it's for that..."

Seeing the happiness on Kedar's face, Reena teased him, "Oh, don't start jumping... the contract isn't signed yet... By the way, what will you give me if you get that contract?"

"If I get this film, I will give you whatever you ask for," promised Kedar.

The following Wednesday, Kedar met Sharmaji. After a casual conversation, he came to the point.

"Mr. Dongre, you see, basically, I am a businessman; I'm not from the film line. This is my first venture. So as an experiment, I am planning to do a short film first. If it succeeds, let's do a feature film.

What do you think?"

Kedar had thought that it would be a feature film. Scope for music in a short film would be so little... the film itself would be thirty-forty minutes long... unlikely to have songs, just background music... But hiding his disappointment, he said, "A very good decision Sir. You are absolutely right."

"Good" Sharmaji smiled with satisfaction. "My friend Malhotra had suggested that you should compose music for my film, so I contacted you. Would you be interested? Do you have time?" he asked.

Kedar was impressed with Sharma ji. He had never imagined a big businessman talking to a young man like him; with so much politeness. Kedar did not have the heart to say no to him. Besides, he had decided long ago that any business opportunity that comes along, no matter how small... is not to be missed. So, he accepted that film.

Of course, Reena was the first person he shared the good news with, asking, "Now tell me, what shall I give you?"

"Don't give me anything, but accept my suggestions..."

"Okay. Tell me" Kedar said.

"Change your name."

"...What?" Kedar was shocked with her demand.

"You promised," said Reena. "Just think for yourself, soon you will become a big music director. In the credits of the film, your name would appear as 'Kedar Manohar Dongre'. Isn't it a bit too long?"

"So, how about just- Kedar Dongre, or Kedar Manohar?" asked Kedar.

"I thought of just K. D. - I mean, the name 'K.D.' doesn't give away any information about your religion, caste, mother-tongue or even which Indian State you belong to. I think it would be an advantage to you - any director, producer from any part of India would give you work. I am suggesting this for your own progress..." Kedar didn't reply, so she continued, "And one more thing. I suggest that you should shift to a decent apartment. If a client comes to visit, you can't invite them to your house in that chawl, can you?"

Kedar was shocked to hear Reena's demands.

"I need time to think," he said sullenly. Unexpectedly, the film won an award at a Short Film Festival. Encouraged by the success, Sharma ji decided to produce a feature film and as per his promise, contacted Kedar for composing music for that film.

Kedar felt obliged to keep his promise to Reena. He told his parents about changing his name and moving to his own apartment. Initially, they were hurt by his decision, but agreed after he explained the reasons behind it. "For others I would be K.D, but for you I will always be Kedar. I will keep visiting you from time to time... Don't you worry." His words consoled them. Soon after that, Kedar moved to a new apartment.

In the credits of that feature film, his name flashed on the screen as 'K. D.' - the music composer. Even this film became box-office-hit. Kedar was on cloud nine. He felt Reena was the cause behind his success. He started seeking her advice before taking any decision in his personal or professional life.

After the success of the first film, Kedar got an opportunity to direct music for some other films too. A couple of those films did well, while three or four flopped at the box office. Whatever the reasons of the failure were, it didn't take long for Kedar to be labelled as "flop music director".

Kedar experienced the true nature of *Chitranagari* (the film world)- "Today's hero could be tomorrow's Zero and vice versa." He broke down; slowly, he lost interest in life, in work. Everybody - even Reena - stopped calling him. When Kedar asked the reason, she said that her father had told her that she can meet him only after Kedar is back with a bang. She advised him to focus on his work until then.

Days, months passed by... the advertisements he was getting reduced and his expenses were barely met. He was unable to pay the instalments of the debt he had taken. Kedar tried hard for some assignment, but didn't succeed.

At that time, when he was desperate for work, he got a call from S.L.V Production asking if he could provide music for one of their

Telugu films. To Kedar the words felt like raindrops falling on sun-scorched ground. He agreed without a moment's delay.

∧∧∧∧∧∧∧∧∧∧∧∧∧∧∧∧∧∧∧∧∧

"Sir, madam is calling." the peon said to Kedar and opened the door for him.

"Hello Mr. K.D. ... Please come in... have a seat", a stylish young lady sitting behind the table greeted him with a pleasant smile.

He said Namaste with folded hands. While sitting down, he read the nameplate displayed on the table. It read 'Lakshmi Reddy, C.E.O., S. L. V. Production' written in Calligraphy letters. He kept the file containing his resume and other papers on the table. Lakshmi madam brushed it off and said, "Actually, there is no need for this. We have heard and read about your work. If you agree to our terms and conditions, we will give this contract to you."

Kedar could not believe his ears.

After the experiences of rejection in the last few years, his confidence level had reached to the lowest. So, he asked hesitatingly, "But I don't know anything about your upcoming film. I mean... unless I know... how can I..." "Yes, you are right." said Ms. Lakshmi and narrated the outline of the film's story. It was based on some historical events. Kedar had never given music to that kind of film, yet he decided to take it up as a challenge. After the fee structure, payment mode and schedule etc. were discussed, Madam and he signed the contract. Even the cheque for the advance amount came in Kedar's hand by the time he finished drinking the second coffee. Everything was happening so fast that Kedar couldn't help but to open the envelope in his hand to make sure that the cheque was real...

After thanking Lakshmi madam profusely, he bid farewell to her and got up to leave.

"One minute, Mr. K.D.," she said, stopping him.

"The MD of our company also wants to meet you. So, on his behalf, I have the pleasure of inviting you for dinner tonight, at our home."

"IT'S AN HONOR FOR ME," said Kedar with a smile.

When Kedar reached the address of the house, a servant opened the door to welcome him and asked him to be seated in the living room. Within minutes, MD of SLV Productions - Shri Venkatesh Reddy, Lakshmi Madam and an elderly lady entered.

After a formal welcome, Laskhmi Madam introduced Venkatesh Reddy as her elder brother and the lady as their mother.

"Aren't you Kedar Dongre? I saw you when you were a little boy." The elderly lady smiled sweetly. "How are Manohar-*dada* and Sushila-*akka*?"

??? How does this woman know me, my parents??? Seeing the huge confusion on Kedar's face, both Venkatesh Reddy and Lakshmi Madam were amused.

At last, Mr. Venkatesh Reddy decided to clarify Kedar's doubts. "Kedar, hey, don't be so perplexed... 25 years ago, we used to live in the same Girgaon chawl where you lived. I'm Venki and she is Lakshmi. Remember...? you used to tease her as 'fatsi'- you used to come to our house to eat idli with sugar - we used to play cricket - and after your batting turn was over, you wouldn't field... remember?"

Kedar slowly started to remember. He also reminisced with them.

During the conversation, Venky's mother Sarojamma told him that after Venki's father passed away, she had to vacate the house provided by his office and she had come to live in the chawl with her two children. At that time, Kedar's parents - Manohar-*dada* and Sushila-*akka* - stood by her, supported her. He had helped her in every way as if he was her own brother. She recalled how difficult it was to get the provident fund amount of her husband. But as Manohar-*dada* was working in the same office, he had helped her to procure and organise all the required documents, so that she could get the provident fund money. Soon after that, they moved to Hyderabad.

Venky said, "Mom still remembers those tough days, and the help your parents did. So, we call them once in a while and enquire about their well-being. My mom also feels good after talking to them.

Lakshmi always enquires about you. We got to know from them that you have become a big music director. We also found out that you are currently free, so we both decided to give you a contract for our new film." Venky was talking to Kedar like a best friend. The puzzle of how he got that contract so easily, was solved.

"Let's continue our chat after dinner." Lakshmi called and everyone got up.

∧∧∧∧∧∧∧∧∧∧∧∧∧∧∧∧

Kedar returned to his hotel room after relishing the spicy but delicious Andhra meal. He had a good time with Venky, Lakshmi and Sarojamma, chatting and remembering his childhood days. It was past midnight but he was unable to sleep. He was thinking about himself, his parents and about his past.

"As I climbed each step of success, I was moving further away from *Aai* (mother) and *Baba* (father). *Why did Baba tell Venky that 'Kedar is currently free'? Did Baba know that I was jobless because my films had failed at the box office? Was he giving a hint to Venky? Was he recommending me to him indirectly?*"

"In fact, my career in music is his legacy. Aai had told me once about Baba's love for classical music. He wanted to learn music in his childhood, but could not; because of the poverty of his family. However, he could identify *ragas* only by listening to *ragdari* (classical) music on radio. In fact, Kedar was named after his father's favourite *Raga* - 'Kedar'. He indulged his passion for music by singing *aartis* during the grand Ganapati festival celebrated in their chawl every year and Sai Bhajans at the temple every Thursday. I loved light filmy music, but because of Baba, I had to learn both Carnatic and Hindustani classical music. He used to say, if the knowledge of classical music is thorough, any other form of music can be learned easily... "

"I remember clearly how I had to do *Riyaz* (practice) after school, while other children played on the ground. I hated it. I would get very angry with Baba. But once, my music teacher said, "Kedar, you are a gifted child... how quickly you learn, singing is in your blood." With his encouraging words and Baba's insistence, slowly I took to singing to the extent that I wanted to be a singer by profession. Unfortunately, after an illness, my voice cracked and became so hoarse that my dreams in a singing career ended. I was very disappointed. Aai said, "Hey Kedar, even if you don't become a singer, you can do something related to music, be patient, find a course like that..." - Then I took up a course in sound engineering and got proficient in sound recording, mixing, editing. I got a job in the first company I applied for. My classical music studies complimented my work, and within two years I became the right-hand man of the music director... but all that was of no use ... Finally, it was Baba's recommendation which gave me an assignment... "

Kedar's eyes were beginning to close.

∧∧∧∧∧∧∧∧∧∧∧∧∧∧∧∧∧∧∧∧∧∧∧∧

The next day, from Mumbai airport he headed straight to Girgaon. He was eager to meet his Aai and Baba, to talk to them about his trip to Hyderabad, about his meeting with Venky, Lakshmi and Sarojamma. He wanted to thank his parents because he had got the new movie contract because of them. He wanted to apologize for neglecting them for so many years. Whether Reena approves it or not, he had decided to compel Aai and Baba to shift to his apartment.

He was impatient to reach home, to fall at the feet of Aai and Baba and seek their blessings.

The taxi stopped in front of the chawl. Kedar rang the doorbell of the house. But there was no response. Instead, Kamat *Ajji* (grandma), who was their neighbour, opened the door of her house.

"Who? Kedar? So early?" The sneer in her voice pierced Kedar. But he ignored it and asked,

"What's wrong *Ajji*? Have Aai and Baba gone out? I should have called before coming." Kedar was nervous.

"It would have been of no use. Manohar passed away last week... suddenly...of a heart attack..." Kamat *Ajji* said sadly. "I don't know... How to tell you ... after he died, your Aai couldn't bear the shock, and... Sushila also passed away on the third day after Manohar's demise..." *Ajji* said with a sigh, "Why didn't God take me instead?"

Kedar felt that the world around him was spinning.

"*Ajji*, I really didn't know..." he said in a hoarse voice.

"How would you know? - You weren't even answering the phone. I heard that you have become a big musician...Today all the people from the chawl have gone to the cremation ground for the rituals, to give *Pind*. Go there if you are free..." and she closed the door on him.

... Kedar's head began to throb... he had a sinking feeling in his stomach...

∧∧∧∧∧∧∧∧∧∧∧∧∧∧∧∧

When he arrived at the ground, all the last rites were completed and the *Pind* (rice Balls offered to the soul of the deceased) was being placed. Crows hovered around the Pind, but didn't touch it... It signified that the deceased person had some unfulfilled wish... what could it be?

Kedar was standing there like a statue. The tears of remorse in his eyes begged for forgiveness.

"Aai, Baba, I made a mistake... I don't deserve - even to apologize - I didn't recognise my true well-wishers... Money, fame, and so-called success had blinded me... You didn't have any of this, but you had people, their goodwill; they loved you, respected you. So many people have come here to bid you a final farewell..."

"Baba, I feel ashamed of myself... My knowledge, my sincerity, my previous success of which I was so proud - all that proved worthless - Even those who once praised my music sky-high, hesitated to be associated with me in my difficult times. The future looked bleak and at that time, Venky gave me work – because of his faith in you... he remembered how both of you had stood by his family... He had kept in touch with you, and I? - Despite being your son, I didn't even answer your missed calls... After leaving home, I didn't bother to enquire about you... I have made grave mistakes ... Today I came to ask for your forgiveness... But I arrived too late..." Kedar was crying bitterly.

A few minutes passed and suddenly someone in the crowd touched Kedar's shoulder. "Oh, look at that, the crow has touched the *Pind*..."

Kedar looked up at the crow... "What could have been an unfulfilled wish of Aai and Baba? - To help me achieve success? - To make me understand that money is not everything in the world...? - To teach me the value of relationships? - Or, just to see me one last time?... I would never know... because I have reached too late ..."

The crowd had dispersed, but Kedar was standing there... immersed in deep thought... repenting and looking sadly at the *Pind*...

* * * * * * * * * * * * * * * *

* * * * * * * * * * * *

XII
Detachment

Kusum always had a counter argument with her mother whenever she was asked to do something in a particular way. 'Why should she not play with boys, why did she have to return home before 6 p.m. when her brother could stay out till 8 p.m., why should she learn household chores...' Her mother had a stock answer for every argument. "When you grow up and become a mother, you will know..." Kusum had heard this sentence from her mother innumerable times... She was smart enough to recognise her mother's mood and kept remaining doubts to herself... "So... you don't have an answer to my question... that's why you are not telling..." Kusum would mutter to herself and go to play.

It took many years for her to understand what her mother meant by that profound statement. During that time, she grew up to be a young responsible woman. After getting married; the challenges that she faced while playing various roles - a wife, daughter-in-law, sister-in-law etc. - and running a household were daunting, but she managed it well. After becoming a mother, Kusum took a few more years to understand the deeper meaning of another mysterious sounding phrase, "A woman is a wife for a few moments and a mother for eternity." She had experienced the truth in that statement, while bringing up her cute little babies - looking after them, caring for them, and being there for them all the time ... Just like her own mother had been for her - even in her old age. Kusum realized how much she was attached to her children. Even though they had grown up as mature adults... children were 'her only world'.

^^^^^^^^^^^^^^^^^^^^^^^^

Like every year, this year too Kusum did 'Ghatasthapana' (a ritual followed on the first day of *Navarathri* Festival). She fasted, worshiped, gave offerings and recited 'Nityapathan' (a series of shlokas that are read every day). At the end of the prayer, she always sang her favourite *stotra* which she had heard in 'Nirgun Mandir'. It was very melodious which filled her mind with ecstasy whenever she sang it....

"Ya Devi Sarva Bhuteshu..." she began to sing.

But that day, something was wrong, she didn't feel happy, her voice shivered and she was not singing in tune...

Because, her mind was not in prayer... It was preoccupied with worry, anxiety... She was thinking 'This year, the children are with us to celebrate Navratri, but what about next year's Navratri -? - By then, my daughter would be married and would be in her mother-in-law's house... not with me... My son would go abroad for education... would he come for the festival? How would he manage without me...?

While chanting the hymn, thoughts of her children filled her mind.

"*Ya Devi Sarva Bhuteshu Matrurupena Sansthita...*" (Oh omnipresent Goddess Durga, who has nurtured all beings in the form of mother). As she sang this line, she realized, not the tune of the hymn, but the words... the meaning of the hymn was permeating in her mind...

"O Mother Goddess, I salute your maternal form. You are a symbol of creativity, innovation, protection... You created all beings and you are present in all beings. So, ... are you residing in me too? ... must be... I am sure, you are in me...' Without her knowledge, she stopped singing. Her mind wandered from the prayer; it started a dialogue with the mother Goddess...

"Hey *Devi*, (Mother Goddess), you are the one who has given birth to the universe. You are THE ULTIMATE MOTHER of all the mothers... You have a macro presence in all the life forms... you give them the knowledge of reproduction, nurturing their offspring... but that knowledge is only as much as needed for that species of life... Like, the Microbes and plants' knowledge is limited only to reproduction, they don't need to nurture – they are not even aware of it... But the higher form of life - like birds, animals – not only do they reproduce, but look after their babies and protect them too. I, a human being... I look at myself as an advanced animal form. Like animals, I too gave birth to babies, brought them up, cared for them, protected them... It is only because of your graceful presence in me, that I could fulfil my duty as a mother. I did everything that animals do, but I lack one of the qualities that they have. The quality of 'detachment'. When the wings become strong, the birds let the chicks fly freely- when the babies learn hunting, the animals let them go on their own. Once the young ones are old enough to care for themselves, the animal/bird- mother detaches herself from them... without expecting anything..."

"Hey *Devi*, that is the quality I lack. The quality of 'detachment'. I can't get detached from my children... I know they are capable of flying independently, safely, strongly, and that they can lead life on their own... but ... I am over-involved with my children... I... don't want to let them go..."

"O *Mahamaye* (the mother supreme), I ask for just one boon..."

"Give me the ingenuity to untangle these delicate threads of love and affection. Grant me the strength to bear the pain of unravelling them. Teach me how to be detached... how to live like a dewdrop on a lotus leaf... It touches the leaf but does not stick to the leaf."

"O *Jagat-janani* (Mother of the Universe), give me your blessings."

With tears in her eyes, Kusum continued chanting. She sang the last line "*Ya Devi Sarva Bhuteshu Shantirupena Sansthita...*" (Hey Goddess, you are present in us in the form of peace). Her mind had calmed down. The turmoil of feelings had quietened. She bowed down before the goddess.

"Oh Mumma, you took so much time today for chanting hymns... I was waiting for *Prasad* all this time... By the way, what favour did you ask for? Must be something special..." her daughter asked mischievously.

Looking lovingly at her daughter and placing *prasad* on her hand, she said, "Yes dear... I did ask for some special favour... but I won't tell you, you will know it automatically when you become a mother..."

* * * * * * * * * * * * * * * * * * * *

* * * * * * * * * * * * * * * *

XIII
Su-Vastu

Anand and I had come to Bangalore on a week's leave in search of a house and to inquire about a school for our daughters, whom we had left with my mother-in-law in Pune. It was quite a feat to get it all together in just five days. But as luck would have it, we liked the third apartment shown by the broker. Having completed one task on hand, we then went on a mission to find a suitable school. One school was without a playground, the other was not giving admission in the middle of the year, and yet another was asking for huge donations. We finally found a school we wanted, met the headmistress of that school, showed the previous year's report cards of the girls, ensured admission and returned to Pune victoriously as if we had won a war.

After I narrated our Bangalore trip to my mother-in-law; her only question was, "Anuradha, are there any Marathi people in the neighbourhood?"

"I don't know... I will know only when we go there..." I replied.

∧∧∧∧∧∧∧∧∧∧∧∧∧∧∧∧∧∧

After a month or so, the four of us landed in Bangalore with bags and baggage.

With Anand's help, I set up the house within a week. I was happy because "Everything was in place and there was a place for everything". From the following Monday, the girls started going to school and Anand to the office.

Preparation of their lunch boxes, getting the girls ready for school, waiting for maids - the daily schedule was in place. I used to be free after an hour of post-lunch nap. I would sit on a chair in the balcony until the girls came home from school; sipping coffee and looking at the bungalow across the street in front of our apartment.

After my routine was well set, one day I went out for a casual walk. I saw a vegetable shop and was attracted by the fresh juicy apples. I went straight inside. Forgetting that I was in Bangalore I asked in Marathi, " कशीदलीसफरचदं? (what is the rate of apples?)",

There was a question mark on the face of the vegetable vendor. Then I placed my finger on the apple and asked again. Now he said "Shimla". I gave up the idea of buying apples. As I turned around, the lady next to me asked something. As soon as I heard the word apple, I stopped, realizing that the lady was also inquiring about the apples. "*Noor Aivatu*" the shopkeeper replied. Then the woman turned to me and said in Marathi, " दीडशरेरुपययकेलिोम्हणतोय (He is quoting 150 rupees per kilo.)"

I was so happy. Not about the rate of the apples, but because I met someone who spoke Marathi...

∧∧∧∧∧∧∧∧∧∧∧∧∧∧∧∧

Her name was Seema Subrahmanyam. She was originally from Coimbatore, but her father had worked in Mumbai for many years. She was brought up in Mumbai, so she knew Marathi. She had completed her architecture degree from J.J. College. After graduation, she worked in Mumbai for a few years and then came to Bangalore after marriage. Mr. Subrahmanyam was also an architect and they both had a consultancy firm in Bangalore. The most important information for me was; she lived in a layout near our apartment complex.

Seema was happy that she would be able to revise her Marathi and I was happy that I got a Marathi speaking friend.

The very next Sunday, I invited Seema and Subrahmanyam to our place for dinner. Anand and Subrahmanyam sat in the balcony, kids played in their room and Seema and I chatted while sitting on the sofa in the living room. We didn't realize how quickly the time passed.

"Anu, did you know that the bungalow across the street was designed by your friend?" Anand asked me after they left.

"Oh, is it?" I was happily surprised. That bungalow was the main reason I had chosen this apartment. Anand knew it, so he had given me this special news.

That bungalow and the garden around it looked so beautiful from our balcony. The front veranda overlooked the lawn and trees adjacent to the compound. There was a porch on one side and the Garage attached to out-house was at the end of the driveway. The main house was one and half storeys. Upper storey had only a staircase and one room. The remaining area was a terrace and a sloping roof. It was my 'dream house'.

^^^^^^^^^^^^^^^^^^^^^^^

That day, we had returned from Mysore after the Christmas holidays. As I opened the living room curtains and peeped outside, I was shocked. I had to call her.

"Seema, do you know? the bungalow you designed - it's being demolished." I blurted out.

"Yes, I know". She replied quietly.

"But why?"

"For Vastu purposes..." She told. I had thought she would feel sad, but she was so cool...

"For Vastu...? What do you mean?" I asked.

"Anu, it needs a long explanation... Right now, I'm in a bit of a hurry. I am leaving for a site visit. Shall we meet on Saturday?"

"Will do. Come home. Let's have *Chaipe Churcha*" I said playfully.

Next few days I spent checking with "Google Sir" and tried to gather some knowledge about "Vastu". But the information I found in various sites was so confusing that instead of finding answers, I ended up getting more doubts.

^^^^^^^^^^^^^^^^^^^^^^^

As scheduled, Seema and Subrahmanyam arrived on Saturday afternoon. As soon as we finished tea, I opened the topic of Vastu, and started barraging them with questions.

"Seema, you know, our apartment does not fit the rules of Vastu. Basically, it is not in a straight direction like East – West – North – South, what to do?" There was concern in my voice.

"Hmm, looks like you've met Google Maharaj" Seema said with a smile. I laughed as well.

"Anuradha, I think you will find the answer to your question at the end of the discussion." Subrahmanyam started talking seriously.

"Anand and Anuradha, Vastu Shastra is an ancient science." He went on, "It was written mainly for the construction of temples, many rules were laid down for that. Even today, big temples are built according to Vastu-shastra..."

"But then about the houses..." I asked midway and bit my tongue. 'Don't talk in between,' Anand signalled me with his eyes.

"Yes, there are Vastu rules about designing houses too. Before I say anything further, please remember that what I am going to share with you, is our interpretation of the Vastu rules... So, let me briefly explain the rules along with the logic behind those rules. Is that okay?" We both nodded in agreement.

"For example, the rules state that the master bedroom, store room should be located in the South-West direction, and the kitchen should be located in the South-East direction..."

"Yes, I read that on Google." I exposed my meagre knowledge.

"Good. When we read it, we wondered as to why should it be so? Then realized that hundreds of years ago, our ancestors would have made these rules by observing 'mother nature', which suited their lifestyle," Subrahmanyam went on to say, "For example, in those days, the definition of wealth in the household was to own farmland, have plenty of grain in the storeroom and cattle in the backyard. So, to store and preserve that grain, they chose the South-West direction and to protect it from being stolen, the room adjacent to it was reserved for the head of the family. India being in the Northern Hemisphere, South West direction gets maximum sunlight throughout the year - protecting grains from dampness. So, the South-West corner was reserved for the master bedroom."

"Indeed, the master bedroom location was logical," exclaimed Anand.

"Now let us consider it in today's context. Do we buy grains wholesale and take the trouble to preserve it for a whole year? The answer is 'No'...we buy grains and groceries as and when we need... Do we keep our valuables or jewellery etc in the house? Again, the answer is "No'... because we feel that those are safe in a bank locker... Now tell me how correct is it to insist that the master bedroom should be in the South-West? Similarly, think about kitchen location. Why was South- East reserved for the kitchen? To take advantage of the pleasant morning sunlight when the whole day's cooking was to be done. But we are no more dependent on sunlight for cooking... our houses have electric lights. So even if the kitchen is not in the South-East direction, there is no harm."

We were listening to him attentively.

"The point is; those days the life of people depended on natural light, wind direction, seasons and weather. So, the rules of Vastu were set to suit that way of life. The aim of these rules was to have proper air-circulation and to have plenty of light in the house. But now, we have electricity for light, fans and A.C for air circulation. So, we feel that those rules are a bit out of date. In other words, we feel that it is not necessary to adhere to them in the present times," said Subrahmanyam.

"What you say makes sense." I said thoughtfully. "But I have one more doubt. You talked about houses, but people insist that offices, factories, shops, even pubs should be 'Vastu compliant', how is that?" I doubted.

"Very smart question, Anu. We have our own doubts whether there were that type of establishments during that period. So how could there be Vastu rules for it?" Seema counterquestioned. "Let me tell you about one of our experiences. Once a gentleman from Canada visited our office for consultation about his house in Canada. He had a problematic marriage. The husband and wife did not agree on many things. An Indian friend of his said perhaps there was some Vastu defect in his house". When he came to India for office work, someone gave him a reference, so he came to us for advice."

But would Indian Vastu rules be applicable in Canada too? A fresh doubt popped up in my mind.

"Then?... What did you say?" I asked.

"So, we told him that we had plans to visit Canada during the summer vacation. At that time, we would visit his house and decide what could be done. Then we gave him friendly advice that in the meantime, he should meet our friend who was a marriage counsellor."

"What happened then? Did you go to Canada?" I was curious.

"No, we never had any plans to visit Canada. He was very disturbed so we had told him that - to console him". Seema said with a smile.

"What happened afterwards is interesting. A greeting card came from him the following January. Along with New Year greetings he had written, 'Changes in the house have been cancelled. Problem solved. Thanks for your advice'. It was signed by both - husband and wife. Can you guess what had happened? They had resolved their differences without any alterations in the house... they didn't need any Vastu corrections, but needed behavioural corrections..."

"Ohhh..." I felt so happy for that unknown 'Happily Married' couple!

"Okay, but what was the problem with the house opposite to our balcony?" Anand's question brought me back to the main topic.

Subramanyam replied. "They are from a well-to-do family, having a flourishing business in Bangalore and a farm in their village. It so happened that, for the last two years the crop did not grow well in their farm. He got less than the expected market rate for the product. He had to bear a big loss... Someone told them that there could be some defects in the Vastu of their house in Bangalore. So, to get it corrected, they came to us, because we had designed it. We tried to convince them that their house in Bangalore had nothing to do with the farm-produce of lower quality... It was so, because there had been less rain...Crops did not grow well in other fields also, what about that? ...If there was a defect in the Vastu of their house, how could they get good farm produce for so many years? Vastu was the same then, wasn't it?"

"So, what did those people say?" I asked.

Seema exclaimed, "They had no answer! The thought of Vastu Dosha had entered their brains so deep! Since we disagreed to make any alterations, they went to some other consultant, and now they are demolishing the house and building a new one as per his advice. Now you tell me; can anyone guarantee good rains and good crops every year on their farm, because of their new house? And even if someone gives such a guarantee, should they believe it? After all, it is our job to explain logically to the client, but it is also their job to understand... isn't it true?" Seema sounded very hurt.

"Let it go." Subrahmanyam understood Seema's frustration. "It's human nature - to hold someone else responsible for all the problems, mistakes and failures. Sometimes the blame goes to Nakshatra (celestial stars), sometimes to the birth chart, sometimes to the government and sometimes to religion; and since the last decade – the favourite scapegoat is Vastu... Can you believe, people find fault with Vastu for anything and everything - failing in exams, losing a job, death in the family, share market loss... Whatever the problem may be - *'Vastu'* gets the blame.

I was thinking deeply and was beginning to understand what he was saying.

"Does it mean that the science of Vastu is bogus?" Anand asked a genuine doubt.

"No, not at all. What I want to say is that; happiness and prosperity should not be related to the Vastu of the house. The rules, which were set hundreds of years ago according to the needs of that era, may not give the same results now. In fact, it may cause inconvenience and may not suit today's lifestyle..." replied Subramanyam.

"Understood." said Anand. "Now just out of curiosity, I would like to ask one more question. Is it possible to build a house according to all Vastu - rules?" Anand asked.

"Good question," said Subrahmanyam. "Well... Answer is YES! If the site is a vast open land, maybe the house could be designed according to the ancient Vastu rules. But in present times, the answer is NO! Because most of the residential plots are of limited measurements, and there are byelaws about setbacks, built-up area etc. In multi-storeyed Apartment blocks where there are many units per floor, common walls between the units, how is it possible to comply with the Vastu rules? And for your information, municipal or corporation bye laws don't match with Vastu rules... So, do you get the clear picture?"

There was silence for a while. No one said anything. I once again got up to prepare one more round of tea.

^^^^^^^^^^^^^^^^^^^^^^^^^^

Keeping track of that bungalow's construction, which was being built in compliance with Vastu, became my pastime. Anand used to tease me that I was the 'self-appointed supervisor' of that house!

After performing a grand *Bhoomi Puja*, the actual construction work started. First of all, a small room was built outside the compound wall - on the street - for watchman. It was a temporary room - cement blocks for walls and G I sheet for roof. The watchman, his wife, and two children lived in that room. He worked as a watchman at night and as helper to the mason during the day. The elder child – a boy, must have been attending school as he was seen only during the evenings. The second child was a little baby. After housework, the watchman's wife was seen playing with the baby.

When my maid went on long leave, I asked the watchman's wife - Adilakshmi – whether she would help me with maid's work. She was happy to get this new job which would increase their family income.

With her Hyderabadi Hindi and my Pune type Hindi, our conversation started. She told me that her husband had come to Bangalore from Andhra Pradesh in search of work. As soon as he got the job, the whole family shifted to Bangalore.

Marking of the building - excavation - laying of foundation - the work was progressing fast. After a couple of months wall construction also started, when I realized that there was no space left for the garden, because the new house was being built very close to the compound. I felt very sad that the house would be without that beautiful garden.

By the end of the year, the construction of the house was nearing completion. One day I asked Adilakshmi,

"This construction will be over soon, then what...?"

"I don't know yet, but something will come up." She assured me with a happy smile. She was not worried as much as I was... but then she was always cheerful, I remembered. She used to say that she had so many reasons to be happy. Happy because her husband got a job in Bangalore, happy about the pleasant Bangalore weather, happy that their house had a sheet roof instead of a thatched roof- not only that, but also happy that her husband drank alcohol only on Sundays. She always dreamt of a bright future... Her husband would work as a full-time mason, the baby-daughter would become a school teacher, and the school-going son would become an engineer. Then he would take building contracts, build his own house and so on - her happiness was genuine and endless...

At the end of the month, she broke the news. "Amma, the contractor is a good man. He has given work to my husband on another construction site. We have to leave on Saturday." Suddenly she became very emotional. "But wherever we go, I will never forget you, Amma. You have never treated me like a servant." She folded her hands in Namaste.

They shifted to a new construction site after two days, but remained in my memory forever...

^^^^^^^^^^^^^^^^^^^^^^^

Life continued. We decided not to renew our three-year contract with the landlord when it ended, because the bungalow, which was my main attraction - had gone.

We moved to another apartment. I didn't bother to find out when construction of "that house" was over, had the owner of that house come to live there, had all their problems in family, business and farm been solved, are the people in that Vastu-compliant house completely happy?

I never felt the need to find out, because my attitude towards Vastu had changed. Each one of us wishes to lead a happy life, to live in -"Su-Vastu". But it should also be understood that happiness does not depend on the thickness of the walls, number of windows, direction of the entrance or the design of the house; rather it depends on the attitude of the people living there. Instead of praising or blaming Vastu for the good and bad events that happen in life, one should be able to consciously and thoughtfully figure out how to overcome the difficulties and enjoy life. Happiness comes from inner peace, contentment and acceptance, it has nothing to do with Vastu - If this is understood, any Vastu would become "Su-Vastu".

I was sure that somewhere, in some corner of the city, one such "Su-Vastu" existed...It would be Adilakshmi's house - who sees only the silver lining of a dark cloud. Her shack would not conform to any Vastu rules...

Yet it would be "Su-Vastu"– a Vastu filled with happiness!

* *

* * * * * * * * * * * * * * *

XIV
Gurudakshina (Honorarium to Teacher)

After reaching home from the office, I routinely checked my letterbox for any mails. Most of the time it contained advertisements, leaflets, fliers of some public meeting, or society notices; but once in a while, there was bank notice, or a letter from somebody, so I checked that box every day.

On that Thursday also, I opened the box as usual, picked up the stack of papers and went home. After getting refreshed, I sat down leisurely on the sofa with a cup of tea in my hand, to check the mail. While sifting through it, a bright yellow envelope decorated with *turmeric-kumkum* dots in all four corners caught my eye. It was a wedding invitation. – 'SELVAN Weds SUBHADRA' – it read.

Who was Selvan and who was this Subhadra? I couldn't recall anything about the bride or groom. This piqued my curiosity. So, I opened the envelope before attending to any other mails and started searching for any clue as to why this card could have been sent to me...

The invitation paper was pink on one side and yellow on the other. It was printed in English on one side and in Tamil on the other side. The wedding date was of the following Friday, at Venkateswara temple in Pudukote, Tamil Nadu. Only *MUHURAT* time was mentioned. Maybe they have combined the wedding reception with post-MUHURAT lunch, I thought.

Even after studying the invitation card so carefully, I couldn't find any link to Selvan, Subhadra or any other names printed on the card...Only a few things I came to know: it was a traditional Tamil wedding card, that the invitation had come from Coimbatore; and since my address on the envelope was correct, it was meant for me only. I stretched my memory, but in vain! Then I guessed that it could be from one of my college classmates - as Selvan was a typical South Indian name.

∧∧∧∧∧∧∧∧∧∧∧∧∧∧∧∧∧∧∧∧∧∧∧∧∧

Despite getting 1027th rank in the Common Entrance Test (CET), I didn't get admission for Computer Science in any of the reputed colleges in Maharashtra. Since I was adamant on C. S.; when I got admission in a college in Vellore, Tamil Nadu, in the branch I wanted; I convinced my parents and went to Vellore from Pune. Only after joining the college, I realized that there was only one student from Maharashtra and that was me! All the other classmates were either from Tamil Nadu, Kerala or Andhra Pradesh. This Selvan was probably one of them...

But who? ...

The next day when I got a call from my friend, the riddle was solved.

After a casual conversation- how are you, I am fine, etc., - he asked,

"Hey Manish, I called to ask if you received the wedding invitation."

"Yes... Yesterday I got an invitation, but didn't know it was your wedding card... because the groom's name is written as Selvan." I replied.

Laughing loudly, he said, "I thought as much, - you wouldn't know - that's why I called. That invitation is not for my wedding... It's for Vinod's wedding... Do you remember our college friend Vinod?"

"I remember Vinod, but the card is for Selvan's wedding," I was quite confused.

"That's right... All of us know him as Vinod, but his birth name is Selvan; so the same name is printed in the invitation. Let it be. Are you coming? You just come to Chennai; I will book our bus tickets to Pudukote from there. Let's have a gala time..."

"I can't promise but I will try my best. It's good that you called". I liked the idea of catching up with my college friends. Deciding that I must attend Vinod's wedding, I immediately started writing my leave application.

^ ^

Rajamani was my classmate in Vellore college and also my hostel roommate. After college, he had settled in Chennai and I had got a job in Mumbai, but we were in touch through occasional phone calls. It dawned on me how I got that marriage invitation. Rajamani must have given my address to Vinod. I remembered; he was the one who had introduced me to Vinod.

The first memory I have of Vellore college is the difficulty I had faced in interacting with other students due to the language barrier.

I could understand the lectures in English because they had mostly technical terms. But conversing with classmates was very difficult, mainly because they used to speak in Tamil, or in English. Being from Maharashtra; knowing Tamil was out of question... and although I knew English, I had no practice of communicating in English at all. Due to the fear of making grammatical mistakes, I hesitated to speak even a simple sentence. I was afraid that everyone would laugh at me.

In short, I did not know their languages and they did not speak in the languages I was fluent in - let alone Marathi - but even the national language Hindi.

Among the hundreds of students in the hostel there was only one student I could talk to and that was my roommate Rajamani... my only friend... like an oasis in the desert. He was from Hyderabad, so we spoke in Hindi. Once I asked him if he would teach me Tamil to which he replied that even he does not know pure Tamil. The Tamil he spoke also contained Telugu words. So, to learn pure Tamil, he introduced me to his friend - Vinod.

Even though Vinod was in his final year of engineering, he agreed to teach me Tamil. Vinod, with curly hair and a friendly smile, was a boy with a pleasant personality who would win over anyone at the first meeting. When my tuition started, I expected to learn Tamil from the scratch, that is from the alphabets. But on the very first day he gave me a basic mantra. "Manish, unlike Hindi, Tamil has very few alphabets. For example, one alphabet for (*ka-kha-ga-gha*) one alphabet for (*pa-pha-ba-bha*) etc. You would get confused. You can read written Tamil only if you know the spoken words and you can speak only if you can read, so learn to write and speak simultaneously."

I followed his advice. Then he gave another key-mantra. "Manish, you must keep speaking in Tamil even if people laugh. Just try to understand what made them laugh, correct yourself and improve your speech."

By following both the mantras given by him, I actually got a working knowledge of Tamil within a year. When someone said that despite being a non-Tamil, I spoke good Tamil, I felt very happy. Of course, the credit for that belonged to Vinod. His second mantra benefitted me in two ways. I started communicating reasonably well - not only in Tamil but also in English!

In the final year of engineering, Vinod got the second rank in the University and got admission in the merit list to Presidency College, Chennai for further studies. He was honoured with the "Student of the Year" trophy by our college. Although our in-person meetings became rare after that, he had earned a special place in my heart.

^^^^^^^^^^^^^^^^^^^^^

Next Thursday when I reached Chennai, Rajamani had come to pick me up at the airport. From there we went directly to the bus stand, boarded the bus and reached Pudukote in the night. We stayed at the hotel booked by Vinod.

Rajamani and I continued to chat till late in the night. From that I came to know more about Vinod. After completing his Master's degree, Vinod did his Ph.D. in Mathematics. The University offered him the post of Mathematics Lecturer, but he declined. At present, Vinod conducted classes in Coimbatore for students appearing for CET exams and also provided free coaching for poor students.

^^^^^^^^^^^^^^^^^

The next day we went to the wedding venue early in the morning. Vinod was occupied, so we just exchanged greetings and sat there watching the rituals. The wedding took place in a very simple manner. There was not much of a crowd. The number of relatives also seemed to be less. From Vellore college, only two of us were there. I noticed that one of our professors – Mr. Srivatsan – did *Kanyadaan*. Though very busy, Vinod and his mother took good care of us. We returned to the room after having a meal that was as delicious as the *prasadam* in the temple.

"Have you ever seen a Tamil wedding before?" Rajamani asked.

"No, never had an opportunity," I said.

"How did you like it? - I mean, was it similar or different from the Maharashtrian type of wedding?" he asked. I was not married, but had attended many weddings. I told the similarities and differences like; the lack of *antarpat* during the *Muhurat* time, the bridegroom tying the *mangalsutra* around the bride's neck while she sat on – maybe her uncle's lap - and so on. Then I asked him my doubt, how come I never saw bride and bridegroom speaking to each other? Is it not permitted?"

"Ah, the question of talking does not arise," said Rajamani, after a pause, "Subhadra can't speak. She is deaf and dumb—"

I was momentarily floored by this bombshell. I didn't know how to react.

"– But, - no, - Why... I mean, Is this a love marriage? They say love is blind... In this case, deaf and dumb..." I didn't put it in words, but Rajamani understood what I wanted to say...

"Oh, It's a long story... I must tell you some background before I answer your question..." he said. After a short pause, he composed his words, and began to speak.

"Do you know Manish, why did Vinod change two or three buses to come to college?"

"Yes, I even asked him once, wasn't that inconvenient and time consuming... why he didn't stay in a hostel instead... He had laughed and replied that he utilized the travel time to revise what he had learnt in class. It was like a practical lesson of "time management".

Rajamani smiled. "What he told you is true, but only partially... Anyway, it's typical of Vinod to answer questions convincingly, without revealing the whole truth...

"So, what's the whole truth?" I asked curiously.

"So... apart from the 'time management', there was another important reason." Rajamani said.

"Simply put, he couldn't afford it!... When Vinod was in the ninth grade, his father passed away. There was no pension nor any savings. So, his mother had to work in several houses as a cook, to keep the fire burning in their own house... He was aware of her hardships, so he too worked part-time, after college, and helped with the household expenses."

"But how could he afford college education with that meagre income?" I asked.

"True ... it was not enough... but be patient Manish, there is more to Vinod's story". Rajamani continued. "Now you might think, how do I know all these details...It's because; when in school, Vinod was my elder brother's classmate. He used to come to our house very often. After his father's demise, Vinod was about to drop out from school. My father thought that a brilliant boy like him should not leave school. So, my father paid his fees. In the SSLC examination, he came first in our school. His teachers wanted him to study further - But what about the money? Then the Headmaster suggested him to approach Rotary clubs and apply for educational support."

So, Vinod sent his request letter to the Rotary clubs, along with the recommendation letter from the school Headmaster. After seeing his marks, one of the Rotarians from a club offered to sponsor his full education, and also arranged for his college admission in Vellore. So; every year, at the annual Rotary function, the President of that Rotary Club gave a cheque to Vinod for his college fees. There was no looking back once he joined the college. He was always a rank student. As you already know, he came out with flying colors in the University.

"Yeah, I remember, he had got second rank," I said.

"And now the 'side' story... you know, Rotary organizes health check-up camps, programs for school children or some other charity projects. Vinod used to go there as a volunteer."

"But between college and work, how could he find time?"

"Once I asked him the same question. He said, "Oh, time... I use my relaxation time to go there. It's called "win-win". They get a volunteer, and I get satisfaction from helping the needy. It is also a great opportunity to express my gratitude to those who help me through Rotary."

With every bit of new information that Rajamani told me, I was more and more fascinated. But I couldn't understand what all this had to do with his marriage.

Rajamani further said, "Do you remember Srivatsan sir from our college? Vinod was his favourite student."

"Yes, I remember. He taught us Physics in the third year. But why did he do the *"Kanyadaan"* ritual today?"

"Be patient Manish. I told you it's a long story…" He picked up the thread. "Once it so happened that Vinod met Srivatsan Sir in one of the Rotary Projects and on that day; from other Rotarians he learnt that Srivatsan Sir was the one who had taken the financial burden of his education… He had insisted that he would sponsor Vinod's fees every year, but his name should not be declared to the beneficiary… Vinod was overwhelmed with sir's kind gesture, and wanted to thank him profusely but respected his wish of remaining anonymous.

So, neither Sir uttered a word about financial assistance, nor did Vinod… But his respect for Sir increased a hundredfold. Rotarians were familiar with Vinod and they liked him because of his helping nature. In one of the blood donation camps, he came to know that Srivatsan sir was unmarried because his younger sister was deaf and dumb. Every marriage proposal got rejected for that reason… One girl expressed bluntly that she was afraid; that his sister would remain unmarried, she would never get a match…and they would have to take care of her sister-in-law for the rest of their life…'

After listening to this, Vinod became very serious. – I don't know whether he consulted his mother, but the very next day he went to Srivatsan sir's house, and straightaway asked for his sister's hand. Sir was surprised. He said, "Oh Vinod, she, - is deaf and dumb - from birth - you haven't even seen her, - and yet - "

"Yes, sir, still, I want to marry her, sir, and yes, I'll meet her now- if you permit".

Then, in his usual charming style, he said, "…And sir, I am not worried about her being a specially-abled person…There is a bright side to it... We won't have arguments after marriage and the house will always be peaceful..." After seeing the genuine smile on Vinod's face, Sir didn't ask any further questions.

"- And thus, the wedding of Vinod and Subhadra was consummated today." Rajamani concluded Vinod's story in the style of a storyteller.

I was so overwhelmed that I had no words to respond.

∧∧∧∧∧∧∧∧∧∧∧∧∧∧∧∧

Rajamani was going to stay there for a couple of more days, but I had to reach Mumbai the next day. So, I had booked the night bus which would reach Chennai in the early morning of next day so that I could catch the afternoon flight to Mumbai.

When we got down from the Autorickshaw, we couldn't believe whom we saw... Vinod had come to the bus stand to see me off.

"What are you doing here on your wedding night?" Rajamani asked him teasingly.

"Night is still young my friend..." He replied, "And it will still be there... but you both and especially Manish, has travelled from so far to attend my wedding... Thank you so much Manish...."

He said sincerely, hugging me.

"You don't have to thank me Vinod, it was my pleasure..." Though I was feeling awkward to ask, my curiosity took charge of me. "But, can I ask you a question? Will you give me a true answer? No beating around the bush..., huh?" I said in one breath.

"Well, - ask," he said with a smile.

" – Why - did you marry a girl like Subhadra? Is it just to have peace in the house? Or is there some other reason?"

I finally asked the question that was bothering me.

"Rajamani seems to have told you many things about my marriage," he said. "Manish, - then you must know how much Srivatsan sir had helped me. Not only did he support my education financially, but in college, he was also my guide, mentor... And the most important thing was, never did he flaunt it anywhere. I felt very sad that such a godly man should face problems in his marriage. I felt that he - who had uplifted my life, should be able to enjoy his life also... I thought I should take the responsibility of Subhadra off his shoulders ... I then discussed it with my mother. Thankfully she also agreed... Marrying Subhadra is my *Gurudakshina* to Srivatsan sir."

On his face, there was a smile of satisfaction.

I smiled too. I was lucky to have an exceptional human being as my friend!

I remembered the sacrifice of Eklavya – who had paid a unique *Gurudakshina*... by cutting off the right thumb...

For me, Vinod was the modern day Eklavya...

* * * * * * * * * * * * * * * * * * * *

* * * * * * * * * * * * * * *

XV
Periwinkle

"Molly, can I ask you a question?" asked Jenny, entering the college gate with a graceful turn.

"Yes, go ahead —" I said.

"Do you know Venky in my class? He says that Indian people's names have a meaning - like his name is the name of some important God."

"Yes, that is the name of Lord Venkateswara, but what about it?" I asked.

"So, does your name also mean anything?" Jenny asked her doubt.

"Yes, it does... I thought, you are going to ask me a very difficult question..." I said with a smile. My name is the name of a white, sweet smelling, beautiful flower. It has long —"

Interrupting my sentence, Jenny exclaimed, "I know, I know, it's a flower called Jasmine, you wear garlands of that in your hair... Venky had told me..." Jenny was delighted to recognize the flower. She was a botany student and flowers always attracted her.

"Yeah... I mean...your guess is right and... wrong," I said.

"Hm... I don't understand...Don't play riddles!" said Jenny, with a question mark written large on her face.

"Let me explain. My name does mean Jasmine, right. But I am not named after 'that' popular jasmine flower which blooms on a bush. This jasmine blooms on the top of tall trees."

"Oh!" Jenny exclaimed. I continued, "All over India, that tree is known as the 'Indian cork-tree'. However, in my mother-tongue - Kannada; it's called "Akash Mallige". Akash means sky and Mallige means Jasmine. That tree grows very tall, as if touching the sky and its flowers are white and fragrant like jasmine... So, *Akash-Mallige* means Sky Jasmine, the Jasmine that blooms in the sky!! "

"Wow...!" Jenny exclaimed. She was listening to me intently.

"And can I tell you something more interesting? "*Akash-Mallige*" is my mother's most favourite tree. During her late pregnancy, the tree was in full bloom, so she named my twin brother - AKASH meaning Sky and me as *MALLIGE* meaning Jasmine," I said with a smile.

"How interesting, your mother seems to be quite the romantic. So, Molly, henceforth, should I call you Molige?" Jenny was truly amused to hear such a long explanation of my simple name.

"Don't bother. Molly is fine." I replied. Jenny giggled as we reached the university parking lot. From there, she went to her lecture hall and I went to the library.

∧∧∧∧∧∧∧∧∧∧∧∧∧∧∧∧∧∧∧

Although there was a computer screen in front of my eyes, I was not looking at it, my mind was wandering. I was remembering how my life had changed in the last few months...

Through a student exchange program, I had an opportunity to come to Frankfurt. When I came to know that our group of six students would be going to Germany instead of America, my father had specifically told me that, even if I was selected in the interview to go to Germany, I should refuse it.

But I was stubborn. Somehow, I convinced him and thus came to Germany. Before leaving India, I learnt German by listening to CDs, reading books and taking lessons. But after coming here, I realized how inadequate that knowledge was. In my host family, only Jenny spoke English. Everyone else used to communicate with me in broken English and gestures. I felt totally lost in that place because, not only the language, but the climate, the food, the mannerisms; even the flora was different. Maybe I should have listened to my father, I thought very often.

I was trying to adjust. But I felt the same even after two months of coming to Germany. In fact, it was the first time that Jenny and I had talked casually. It was great. I felt as if a delicate thread of friendship connected us.

Then onwards, we both started chatting on random topics as well. She even shared her fondest dream of coming to Pune after getting her degree and learning authentic Iyengar yoga.

Soon the winter season was over. The spring season arrived. The barren trees came to life. Buds appeared on some trees; tender leaves appeared on others. I was fascinated to witness this change.

Once Jenny said, "Molly, Venky and I are going for a day's picnic to the nearby forest, will you join us?"

"No, two is company, three is a crowd?" I teased her with a smile.

"Don't worry about that. Venky and I went last year too. You will be here only for a year, so I think you shouldn't miss the chance to see every season of the year. Come on... Join us." After being invited so lovingly, I couldn't say no.

The following Sunday, Jenny parked her car in an open field outside the village and from there, the three of us walked further into the forest. The fresh green groundcover was glistening with dew-drops on it, the tender leaves of the trees had cast tiny shadows, and the thin rays of the sun had penetrated the trees to brighten up the whole atmosphere... it looked like a dreamy, beautiful painting; created by mother nature. And the best part was; at that moment, Jenny, Venky and I were a part of that picture – an exhilarating experience indeed...

Breathing in the cool fresh air and enjoying the scenic beauty of the forest, I was walking as if in a trance...

"Molly, look over there, - on your right side - periwinkle" I looked in the direction Jenny pointed and I couldn't believe my eyes... Wow... a large bed of *Sadaphuli* -periwinkle flowers ... (*Sadabahar in Hindi*)

I stood there staring lovingly at the flowers, without blinking my eyes.

"Molly, what happened? Why did you stop?" asked Jenny, looking back.

"Jenny...I met my dear friend" I said in an overwhelmed voice. "Well, I am so happy I joined you today. Thank you so much, Jenny."

I was so excited that I hugged her. Jenny was puzzled but both of them - Venky and Jenny were amused and smiling to see me so excited...

I returned home as if floating in the air... I stayed up till late night and opened my heart to Jenny. I spoke about me, my family, our Davangere house and the garden around it.

"My mother was very fond of gardening. So, my father had bought a plot of land - the largest in the colony - with a row of Indian Cork trees facing the plot. They had built a small house leaving plenty of space for a garden. There were several flowering plants in the front yard and fruit-bearing trees in the backyard. My mother had developed a nursery of plants as well and she would give saplings to anybody who showed interest in her garden. Our neighbours used to call our house 'garden house' because there was more area of garden than for the house. My mother used to spend all her free time tending the garden and I loved to watch her. To please my mother on her birthday, once I had brought a Periwinkle plant that had grown in the roadside footpath."

Jenny listened without interrupting me, so I continued...

"Where should I plant it?" I asked. Mother pointed to a corner of the garden. There it caught on very well and soon began to flower. Although it had a bitter smell, I didn't mind. I loved periwinkle because it would flower every day. It had no demands - like daily watering, regular fertilizer or spray of insecticides... I liked the simplicity of it. Slowly, periwinkle became my best friend and that corner of the garden became my special corner. I used to study there. Though I was an introvert by nature, my dear periwinkle knew everything about me, my school pranks and later college secrets. In fact, she was the first one with whom I shared the news of my interview, then getting selected and going to Germany. And before leaving, I promised her that I would return soon..."

I was feeling homesick. Jenny could understand that. She just patted me on the back. After a brief pause, I said,

"I was missing my friend a lot. But I met her today... only because of you". Seeing me emotional, Jenny said, "So, now onwards you have two friends in Germany, Periwinkle and Jenny. Okay?" And she smiled beautifully.

Periwinkle had inadvertently created a delicate yet strong bond between me and this unfamiliar land...The rest of my year in Germany went smoothly.

^^^^^^^^^^^^^^^^

I returned to Davangere and completed my college education. Jenny called me once in a while. She told that she had married Venki after graduation. She taught Botany at the University and apart from that, conducted German classes for Indian students. I was very happy when she said that she remembered me often and especially when Periwinkle bloomed. She was waiting for an opportunity to come to Pune and learn Iyengar Yoga.

Ever since I returned from Germany, the travel-bug had bitten me. I wanted to visit different countries and study their culture. But my father refused. On the contrary, he wanted me to settle down in marriage. One day he asked me "What do you think of Sharad Santoorkar? He lives in our own colony". Although I was in no hurry to get married, I knew that I had to marry someone – someday.

So, I just thought over my father's proposal. Sharad was an officer in the Indian army. That means he would be transferred to different cities. So, I would be able to live in different regions of India, if not in different countries. My dream of travel, meeting people from different communities would be partially fulfilled at least...I thought wisely, and accepted the proposal.

After marriage I started liking Sharad. He was a cool person and had a well- balanced attitude. Growing up in the Army campus made our children true Indian citizens. Every three years, Sharad got a posting to a different base, and we would shift to a new army campus. New house, new neighbours. But no matter where the house was, I made sure that periwinkle always bloomed in its premises.

I used to visit *Aai* (mother) and *Anna* (father) whenever I could find time from Sharad's transfers and children's school schedule. When Sharad got a promotion as 'Major', we got bigger quarters. Also, there were servants to help. So, we invited *Aai, Anna* and Sharad's Mummy-Daddy to visit us. They were impressed to see the overall atmosphere in the army campus, how much Sharad was respected by his juniors, the disciplined behaviour of our children and how all the families lived like a joint family. They were happy to know that in times of peace, jokes, banter, parties would go on, but in times of war, everyone would support each other.

∧∧∧∧∧∧∧∧∧∧∧∧∧∧∧∧∧∧∧∧

Life had become a routine. Years passed by. Our son got commissioned in the Army, and daughter left to study M.S.in the US.

As Sharad's retirement approached, we started thinking seriously about where to settle down after retirement.

Of course, our first choice was Bangalore. It was a big city, easily accessed by air, railway or by road, had a cosmopolitan population, had many other facilities and it was convenient in all aspects. We came to know that a builder had plans to build an apartment complex, especially for defence personnel in Bangalore. We were aiming to book an apartment in that complex but we had limited savings. So, to raise the additional amount, we thought of discussing with Sharad's parents who had settled in Canada with their elder son; and check whether they are agreeable to sell their house in Davangere.

So, we decided to visit Bangalore. But before that, I wanted to visit Davangere to meet my parents. It had been three or four years since I had seen *Aai and Anna*. Besides, I was also very curious to see *Akash baiya*'s new housewhich he had built by demolishing our previous house.

Although Akash and I were twins, our similarity was limited only to our date of birth. He would always go to touch the sky while my feet were firmly rooted in the ground. When we were kids - even though he was only five minutes older than me - he would insist that I call him *Akash baiya*. The memory made me smile.

As I expected, *Akash baiya*'s new house was built in a very modern way. He had bought the adjacent plot, hired a landscape architect and created a Japanese garden there. I went around the beautiful garden but was unable to find what I was looking for.

"Your garden is nice, but where is my 'periwinkle corner'?" After walking around the garden, I asked *Akash baiya*.

"What are you saying, Malli? - Your periwinkle in the Japanese garden?" He said sarcastically. "And anyway, do you know what Periwinkle is? – It's just a useless plant- neither fragrant, nor decorative – how can it fit in a Japanese garden...It's a lowly – wild plant –that grows by the roadside-" He continued to condemn periwinkle more and more, but I didn't want to listen. I remembered the sad faces of my parents when I met them before going around the garden. Weird thoughts crossed my mind...

'Oh, does *Akash baiya* think that Aai-Anna are as useless as periwinkle? Is that why, Aai-Anna's small room is adjacent to the outhouse? – Is that why they are restricted to that room? Though the thoughts disturbed me, they explained Aai-Anna's unusually quiet demeanour. My heart was broken, but mind was overworking. I wanted to find a solution...

Before leaving for Bangalore, we visited Sharad's elderly uncle and aunt at their daughter's house. Uncle told us that his daughter and the son-in-law had taken them in only after uncle tranfered his assets in his son-in-law's name, and still they were treated like destitute...

Both Sharad and I were so sad, upset and lost in our thoughts, that we returned home in total silence.

Finally, Sharad brought up the subject. "Malli, I have something on my mind. Can I share it with you?"

"Sure, go ahead," I said.

"Hmm... it's only if you agree to my suggestion wholeheartedly... Should we settle down in Davangere instead of Bangalore?" he asked.

"How could you read my thoughts?" I said with a broad smile. "You spoke what was on my mind too... And I want to suggest something else also - of course only if you agree -"

Interrupting my sentence, he said, "Are you mimicking me? Let it be, tell me what you wanted to say."

"As you suggested, let us drop the idea of the Bangalore Apartment. Furthermore, let us renovate your Davangere house. We can utilise our savings for that... and then shift Aai, Anna, your Uncle and Aunt there. We can hire a cook and a helper for them. Let's make your house a paradise for them..."

"Yeah, I'm in total agreement with you," Sharad said earnestly.

"And next year, when we shift here, let us accommodate other senior citizens - like Aai-Anna - to live in this paradise. I want to see them cheerful until their last day... I don't care if *Akash baiya* cannot spare even a square inch for my dear periwinkle in his garden; I am going to grow a whole garden -full of periwinkle - *Sadaphuli* – the one that would always be in bloom ..."

I stopped talking. My voice choked; my eyes were full of tears. My *Sadaphuli* had given me a purpose... it was going to make the rest of my life meaningful.

Sharad lovingly held my hands. I smiled at him.

My eyes visualised the vast expanse of periwinkle that Jenny had shown me years ago... and the happy faces of senior citizens that resembled the blooms of periwinkle!

* * * * * * * * * * * * * * * * * * *

* * * * * * * * * * * *